The Same Stuff as Stars

Angel Morgan needs help. Her dad is in jail, and her mother has abandoned Angel and her little brother, Bernie, at their great-grandmother's crumbling farmhouse. Grandma spends most of her time wrapped in a blanket by the wood stove and can't care for the children. That's left up to Angel, even though she's not yet twelve.

In this dreary world of canned beans and peaches, of adult worries and loneliness, there is only one bright spot—a mysterious stranger who appears on clear nights and teaches Angel all about the stars.

★

The Same Stuff as Stars

★

Other books by Katherine Paterson

Preacher's Boy

KATHERINE PATERSON

★

The Same Stuff as Stars

★

OXFORD
UNIVERSITY PRESS

OXFORD
UNIVERSITY PRESS

Great Clarendon Street, Oxford OX2 6DP

Oxford University Press is a department of the University of Oxford.
It furthers the University's objective of excellence in research, scholarship,
and education by publishing worldwide in

Oxford   New York

Auckland   Cape Town   Dar es Salaam   Hong Kong   Karachi
Kuala Lumpur   Madrid   Melbourne   Mexico City   Nairobi
New Delhi   Shanghai   Taipei   Toronto

With offices in

Argentina   Austria   Brazil   Chile   Czech Republic   France   Greece
Guatemala   Hungary   Italy   Japan   South Korea   Poland   Portugal
Singapore   Switzerland   Thailand   Turkey   Ukraine   Vietnam

Copyright © 2002 by Minna Murra, Inc.
Published by special arrangement with Clarion Books,
an imprint of Houghton Mifflin Company

Excerpt from 'Take Something Like a Star' from *The Poetry of Robert Frost*
edited by Edward Connery Lathem. Copyright 1949, © 1969 by Henry Holt and Co.,
© 1977 by Lesley Frost Ballantine. Reprinted by permission of Henry Holt
and Company LLC.

Database right Oxford University Press (maker)

First published 2002
First published in the UK by Oxford University Press 2003
First published in this UK educational edition 2006

British Library Cataloguing in Publication Data available

ISBN-10: 0 19 832632 7
ISBN-13: 978 0 19 832632 8

1   3   5   7   9   10   8   6   4   2

Printed in Malaysia by Imago

★

This book is for my sisters
Helen and Anne
as token payment on the family debt
Elizabeth
who never let me run away from home
and
Caroline
who loved our brother, Ray

★

Contents

Wishing on a Star

When she heard the first yelp, Angel was at the sink washing the supper dishes. She thought the sound had come from the couple in the upstairs apartment beginning their nightly fight. She was late washing up, having waited supper, hoping that since it was Friday, Verna would get home in time for the three of them to sit around the table and eat together like a family.

It was when the yelp turned into crying that she realized where it was coming from. "Bernie!" Angel raced down the hall to the living room, not even stopping to wipe the suds off her hands. Bernie sat on the rug, whimpering and staring at the couch. Flames were dancing up from a worn cushion. "What are you doing?" she yelled, slapping the open box of kitchen matches from his hand. The matches scattered over the rug. "You want to kill us all?"

"I just wanted to see if it would really burn," he said, still whimpering.

She raced back to the kitchen and grabbed the dishpan, not stopping to take out the dishes before she ran back to the fire. Angel sloshed the dirty dishwater over the flame. It sizzled angrily and died. She stood watching the steam, her heart pounding. When she could speak, it was a yell. "I swear, Bernie Morgan, how old are you?"

"Seven," he muttered.

"Well, you act like you're two." She knelt, putting the dishpan down, so she could pick up the matches and put them back in the box. Her hands were shaking. "Now I'm going to put these away, and don't you ever touch them again, you hear me?" She stood up. "You can bring the dishpan to the kitchen for me."

He followed her down the hall, rattling the dishes against the side of the plastic pan. "Don't tell Mama," he said.

"It won't matter if I tell Mama or not. The minute she comes in here she's going to smell smoke and know something happened. I swear you're going to run me crazy if you don't kill us both first." On tiptoe, she put the matchbox on the highest shelf she could reach. Bernie plumped the dishpan down on the floor. "Where do you think you're going?" she asked his retreating back.

"To watch TV. You're too mean to talk to."

She put the dishpan back into the sink and marched down the hall. Snatching the remote out of his hand, she threw it on the sodden couch. The whole room stank.

"Quit it!" he said.

"Do you think you can just sit there on the floor watching TV like nothing happened? Come on." She grabbed Bernie's hand, dragging him to his feet. "We'll go out and wait for Mama to come back, and then you can just tell her yourself what a fool thing you did."

He set his feet and tried to wriggle his hand out of her grasp, but Angel was wiry, and the boy was no match for her. Still, by the time she had dragged him out the heavy front door and onto the porch, her fury was spent. He was always into things. She should have been watching more closely. That's what Mama would say when she came home. *Just where were you, Miss Angel Morgan, while your brother was trying to burn down the house? Huh? Where were you?*

And where are you right now, Verna? Did you forget tomorrow is Saturday and we have to make an early start? Angel let go of Bernie's hand and went over and sat down on the edge of the porch, her feet on the top step. It was nicer outside than in the hot, smelly apartment. The night had absorbed some of the stickiness of the summer day. "Sit down, Bernie," she said gently, and patted the spot next to her. He stayed where he was. She could almost feel the stiffness in his little body. He was still angry with her and scared by what he had done.

In the strained stillness between them, she could hear the hum and honk of city traffic a few blocks away. Their own street was quiet and dark. Someone—she would have suspected Bernie if she'd thought he could throw a rock that far—had broken the single streetlight weeks before, and the city had yet to replace the bulb. Burlington didn't seem to worry about fixing things in this neighborhood—just about poking around trying to catch drug users. The large houses, most, like theirs, divided into two or more decaying apartments, squatted like old women, staring at each other, fat and sullen, across the narrow, potholed street. She hated this place, but it was better than some they'd lived in, certainly better than foster care.

Then she saw the star. Just one, through the cloudy night sky, but blinking like a friend above the house across the way. It was like a sign. Like a promise that things were going to get better.

"Look, Bernie," she said. "With the streetlight out, the star looks really bright."

"So?"

"So wish. Wish on the star, Bernie."

"I don't want to."

"You got to."

"How come?"

"'Cause I told you to, okay?"

"You can't make me. You're not my boss."

"Bernie, we got to do it." She craned her neck around to look at him. He was standing where she'd left him, his small back pressed against the screen door. "How else are we going to get Daddy home?"

"I don't want him to come home."

"Yes, you do. C'mon, Bernie. *Wish.* 'Star light, star bright, first star I see tonight. I wish I may, I wish I might, have the wish I wish tonight.' Now, go on. . . . I wish Daddy would soon—"

"I wish that stupid guy would *never never never* come home."

"Bernie!" She jumped to her feet, hands on her thin hips. "Take that back! You don't wish any such thing!"

"Do, too. I hate him. I never want to see him again."

What was Angel to do? Bernie had messed up the star wish, and there weren't that many first-star wishes you could make in the middle of Burlington, Vermont. If the streetlight hadn't been broken, they probably wouldn't have had this chance. And now Bernie had ruined it—canceling out her wish with his terrible one.

"I'm never going to speak to you again as long as I live, Bernie Morgan."

"Good. Then you can't boss me around no more." He stuck his thumb into his mouth, but just as he turned to go back into the apartment, the lights of a vehicle turning into their dead-end street swept across the yard across the way. "It's Mama!" Bernie said.

"Wait," she cautioned, standing on the porch, squinting her eyes to try to see past the headlights. It was the old pickup, going too fast for this short street, making a wide turn into the driveway. It passed by the waiting children. Beside the kitchen entrance it slammed to a stop. Bernie, as though he'd forgotten he was in big trouble, raced down the drive to meet Verna as she got out of the cab of the truck. Angel followed behind.

"What are you doing up, boy?" Verna's voice was thick but not unkind, so maybe she hadn't drunk too much.

"We was waiting for you," Bernie said.

If they all went in through the kitchen, maybe Verna wouldn't even go into the living room. Maybe everything could be put off until after tomorrow. Angel didn't want to mess up Saturday morning. Not after Bernie had ruined the star wish. Verna would have to know eventually, but maybe they could get through tomorrow morning without a blowup.

★   ★   ★   ★   ★

Angel undressed in the living room by the light of the bare bulb in the hall. It wouldn't do to turn on the living room light and attract Verna's attention. She took the cushions off the couch. The wet one really stank. If she turned the burned side over, though, maybe it would be days before Verna noticed. For tonight she'd hide them between the back of the couch and the wall. Maybe by morning it would be dryer and not so smelly. She yanked hard and lifted up the couch seat, turning it into her bed. Mama had told her not to leave the sheets on, but Angel usually did. It was so much trouble to put them on every night, and Verna hardly ever noticed, whatever she might say.

Angel took off her clothes and laid them on top of the dresser in the closet. In the morning she'd put them away properly. She got her pillow off the closet shelf and pitched it onto the couch. Then she fumbled in the top drawer of the dresser for her nightshirt, really just one of Verna's old T-shirts, and slipped it over her narrow shoulders.

She could hear the murmur of Verna's and Bernie's

voices coming from across the hall. They sounded almost cheerful, so Bernie hadn't told Mama what he'd done. That was for sure.

As she settled down under the rough sheet, she remembered the dishes. They weren't even soaking. The leftover macaroni and cheese would be stuck on like cement. She ought to get up and finish washing them and putting away the leftovers, but she couldn't make herself. She was tired. Besides, Mama had been drinking. Even though tomorrow was Saturday, she'd want to sleep in as long as possible. Angel would have time to clean up in the kitchen *and* give Bernie his breakfast before Verna was up.

★ ★ ★ ★ ★

Angel made sure the water was boiling hard before she poured it on the heaping spoonful of powdered coffee. She stirred it well and then carried it into the bedroom.

Verna was sprawled across the width of the double bed. Her bleached hair with its dark roots was damp with sweat. Her face, which could really be pretty when she fixed herself up, looked tired and unhappy even when she was asleep. Whenever Angel got mad at Verna, she tried to make herself remember how hard Verna's life was, had always been. Angel and Bernie had only been in foster care twice, and they had been back with their mother for almost a whole year. Verna had never lived with her real mother or father. She'd spent time in eight different foster homes and a group home before she ran away and married Daddy. She'd hadn't even finished high school.

How could anyone expect her to know about being a good mother? She couldn't remember having a mother of her own.

"Mama?" Angel said. "I brought you some coffee."

"Oh, crap, don't tell me it's morning already."

"It's past eight, Mama. If we don't get there before ten . . ."

"Okay. Okay. Get Bernie something to eat and get his clothes on. I'll be ready in a minute." She flopped over on her stomach and put her pillow over her head.

"We've already had cereal, Mama, and Bernie got himself dressed." He'd picked out his own T-shirt and pants—not the ones Angel would have chosen, but she wasn't going to fight that battle this morning. She was hardly speaking to him since last night's near disaster.

"Well, give me a minute to get my own clothes on." The pillow muffled her voice. "You can get him washed up. I'm sure he needs that."

Angel put the coffee down on the bedside table. The TV was blaring cartoon noises from the living room. She went to the door.

"Bernie, Mama said for me to get you washed up. You need to turn the TV off."

"I thought you wasn't speaking to me no more," he said prissily.

"*Weren't*. Weren't speaking to me. Oh, shut up and come here. I got to wash your face."

"No."

"Bernie, don't be a baby. You're seven years old."

"I can wash my own face."

Angel sighed. He wouldn't do it right. He'd just swipe the rag across his nose. He wouldn't get any of the dirt off. She went into the bathroom, brushed her teeth, and washed her own face more carefully than usual to make up for not washing Bernie's.

Bernie was still on the living room floor staring at the TV, his mouth open like the beak of a baby bird waiting for the worm to drop in. His body blocked the closet door. "Move," she said. He shifted his legs without taking his eyes off the screen.

Bernie was watching entirely too much television. Angel knew about the evils of too much TV for kids. It was like getting only sugar in your mental diet—like not eating all the five major food groups. Ms. Hallingford, Angel's fifth-grade teacher, was big on the major food groups. She'd also said TV could be a really serious hindrance in a child's mental development, in the same way not eating right could stunt your physical growth. Angel grabbed the remote and punched the red button.

"Hey!"

"Go wash your face before Mama comes in here and beats your bottom shiny!" She shouldn't threaten him, she knew, but sometimes it was the only way to make him behave.

"I hate you," he said, stomping out of the room and

down the hall. Angel waited until she could hear the water running before she yanked open the closet door.

Under the clothes rod, pushed back against the wall, was a partly purple dresser. Verna had started painting it, but she'd never finished covering up the old green paint. Angel got out her best jeans and a clean T-shirt, the pink one, so Daddy would know she'd tried to please him. He always said he liked to see his angel girl wearing pink.

She was zipping up her pants when Verna appeared in the door. "Ain't you kids ready yet?"

"Almost." Angel began hurriedly to fold up the sheets.

"Here," said Verna, grabbing the tab and heaving the couch back into place. "Bernie!" she yelled. Bernie stuck his head in the doorway. His face was as dirty as if it had never seen the back of a washrag. "Just look at you. And you, too, Angel. Take off them jeans. Least you could do was put on a dress."

"Oh, Mama."

"Don't you start whining. I am seriously *not* in the mood. C'mere, boy. I'll show you how to wash a face."

Angel could hear Bernie howling from the bathroom as she put the sheets in the top drawer and slid a dress off one of the metal hangers. The dress was almost too small, and it didn't have any pockets, but with Verna in one of her moods there was no point arguing. She slipped off her jeans, took the money out of her pocket, and put it in her sock. She needed to be prepared—ever since that time Verna had forgotten and left her and Bernie at the all-night diner. That meant always wearing the apartment key on a string around her neck and carrying enough cash to get a taxi home. It was too embarrassing otherwise, strangers pawing all over you and clucking and threatening to call the cops on your parents.

"Okay," yelled Verna, dragging a still whimpering Bernie down the hall. "I'm leaving," she said on the way down the back steps.

Angel grabbed up her sneakers and ran sock-footed out the door. She could hear Verna grinding the pickup's balky ignition. Halfway to the truck, she realized that she hadn't locked up. She ran back, reopened the door, turned the catch, and slammed hard. By the time she had tested the knob to make sure it had locked, Verna was gunning the motor. Angel raced across the small, weedy yard. She was panting when she climbed up into the cab of the pickup and slid in beside Bernie. The truck began backing down the driveway while she was still pulling the door to. She hurried to fasten Bernie's seat belt and then her own before they turned the corner into traffic.

She sneaked a glance at Verna across Bernie's head. As usual, Mama had forgotten to buckle up. She wanted to remind Verna to fasten her belt, but she didn't. Verna was in such a snit. It was better not to say anything.

★   ★   ★   ★   ★

They were late, so the parking lot was already jammed. Angel leaned forward, anxious. If Verna couldn't find a spot right away, she was apt to just turn around and go home. It was funny. As little as she wanted to come, Angel felt somehow that they had to, that something awful happened those Saturdays they didn't. There was nothing she could put her finger on, just a feeling that they must come, they *had* to come or else. . . . The else part was cloudy but seemed very real to her. Like money they owed somebody and had to pay regularly, or every Saturday there'd be some terrible punishment for their failure. Besides, there was Bernie's awful star wish last night. She'd have to work hard to make up for that.

"I see one!" she cried out.

"Where?" Verna slammed on the brakes, throwing Angel and Bernie forward against their seat belts.

"There—beside the Buick."

"Huh. That ain't wide enough for a kiddie car."

But just then a rusting Pontiac behind them on the other side of the lane began to back out. Verna threw the gears into reverse and screeched back to claim it. "C'mon," she said, hopping out. "We're late."

"I—I gotta put on my sneakers."

"For crying out loud, Angel. You had all morning. Hurry up."

She hurried as fast as she could. "Okay, Bernie," she said, unbuckling his seat belt before opening her door and jumping to the pavement. "Out."

But Bernie had that stubborn look on his face. "I'll give you money for a pack of M&M's if you just come on in."

She could see him weakening, but he still wasn't moving. "And a Pepsi," he said.

"Okay."

"And potato chips."

"No."

He folded his arms across his chest.

"Oh, Bernie. I'm not made of money. Just come on."

Verna was already across the lot. When she reached the door to the building, she turned and yelled, "You kids don't get over here this minute, I'm taking a belt to the both of you."

Bernie scrambled out. Did that mean Angel still owed him the bribe? Oh, well, she'd have to worry about that later.

The Saturday Visit

Verna was signing in at the window when Angel and Bernie pushed open the heavy front door. "'Bout time you two showed up," she said. "Honestly." The woman on the other side half stood up from her chair to peer down over the sill at them. It made Angel feel like she was standing there in her underwear. Too late, she remembered that she hadn't brushed her hair. Not that it mattered. It was ugly hair, dirty blond, straight. She'd cut it herself a couple of weeks ago.

Finally, Verna put down the ballpoint and jerked her head at the children. She shoved her shoulder against the inner door, and the three of them crowded through it into the room and toward the metal detector.

"Purses here," ordered the guard. "All your metal in the tray." Verna handed over her cracked vinyl bag. Angel took the key from around her neck and dropped it into the plastic basket, hoping Verna wouldn't ask her why she was wearing it when it wasn't even a school day, but Verna wasn't paying attention. She was pushing Bernie through the detector ahead of her while the guard did a thorough search of her purse.

Angel followed. The alarm screamed. "Okay. Just a minute, girly. Empty your pockets."

"I don't have any pockets." Her voice was trembling. "See."

"Well, you got metal on you somewhere. Go back. Take off your shoes and hand them here."

The coins in her socks. She'd forgotten about them. She took the socks off, too, and held them out to the guard. He screwed up his face and sniffed. The socks were dirty from when she'd run across the yard. "I got some money in my socks," she mumbled, hoping Verna wouldn't hear.

"You what?" the guard asked loudly.

"Money in my socks," she said miserably.

"Well, get it out and put it in the tray. Jeez. It ain't as if you people don't know the drill by now."

Verna stood on the other side of the detector, squeezing Bernie's arm and looking like a wasp about ready to sting. As soon as Angel got through the detector, Verna grabbed her arm, never letting go of Bernie's in the process. She pushed both children ahead of her through the series of metal doors that opened before them and closed after them on the way to the visitors' room. "Ouch," said Bernie. "Leave go of me. Ouch." He swatted at Verna with his free hand, but their mother just tightened her grip until even Angel wanted to squeal out in protest. She was already humiliated enough, walking barefoot down the corridor and now standing just inside the door of the big room with her shoes and socks in her hand. She didn't need to have everybody see her being dragged by her mother and shoved around like a disobedient cat.

The light in the room was always so bright that she had to blink to keep her eyes from smarting. "Find us someplace to sit, Angel." Verna let go of Angel's arm and pushed her forward into the room.

Other families, the ones that had gotten here on time, had already claimed the tables scattered about the room. She squinted, looking for vacant chairs. Mostly she saw people. Maybe fifty, maybe more. It was hard to tell. They were different sizes and colors, but most of them, especially the women, wore the same sad, tired expression. There were guards all around, making sure none of the visitors were passing drugs or anything else illegal to the inmates. You could pick out the inmates pretty quickly. Nearly all of them were young. They looked more angry than sad. It was summer, so most of them had on cheap jeans and T-shirts. The man nearest her had tattoos up and down both of his skinny arms, like he was trying to be a he-man. He turned around and glared at her. She moved on, making her way through the maze of tables surrounded by gray, unhappy people.

At the far corner of the big room she found two chairs and put a shoe with the sock stuffed in it down on each of them. Her mother was checking in with the attendant, but when Verna looked up, Angel waved her over.

Verna was still holding on to Bernie. Angel barely

managed to pick up her shoe before Verna plunked him
down on one of the chairs. "For chrissake, Angel, put on
your stupid shoes." She handed Angel the other offend-
ing shoe and sock, then sat down herself.

Angel backed over to the wall and slid down to the
floor. She was about to pull on her first sock, the change
jangling away, when she realized she was being stared at.
She looked up into the face of a little boy who, standing
up, was just a little taller than she was sitting down.

"You ain't got no socks on," he said solemnly.

"And you got a great big boogie hanging out your
nose!" she said fiercely.

His eyes widened in fright.

"Boo!" she said right into his face. His mouth twisted,
but before he could begin to cry she whispered, "And
don't you dare cry! Or I'll get you good!"

He turned and fled.

She should have been ashamed. If anyone had tried to
scare Bernie in that room, she would have gone after him.
But she couldn't help it, she was grinning like a jack-o'-
lantern as she finished tying her laces. She stood up, but
she stayed against the wall until the guard brought Wayne
in and led him over to where Verna and Bernie were sitting. Then she made herself join them.

She'd always thought of her daddy as tall and sort of
handsome, but today he seemed shorter than she remembered. Or maybe she was getting taller. Wayne was wearing his long-sleeved plaid shirt. He had tattoos to show

off, if he wanted, but once she had asked him about the needle tracks and he'd never worn a T-shirt or anything short-sleeved since. "Hi, Daddy," she said.

"Well, there's my angel girl," he said, smiling at her. There was something wrong about his smile. Angel couldn't figure it out, except that the smile didn't come from the inside. It was more like someone just twisted up his lips from outside. "You doing good at school?" he asked.

"School's been out for weeks, Wayne. You know that," Verna snapped.

"You lose track of time in here, but you wouldn't know about that." He turned from Verna to Bernie, bending down to try to see Bernie's face. But Bernie was watching his toes swing back and forth so hard Angel could hear his heels banging the chair rung. "Bernie, my man, how goes it?" Bernie didn't even look up.

"Get off that chair, Bernie. Angel, take him somewhere else. I got a few things I got to say to your daddy without . . ."

Angel grabbed Bernie by the hand and started across the crowded room to the opposite corner, where some charity group had put a few worn books and discarded toys for the kids who had to spend their Saturdays in jail.

"Ow," said Bernie. "Quit pulling on me. I'm tired of you and Mama yanking me around. Yank. Yank. Yank. That's all you ever do."

"I'm sorry, Bernie." She really was. It wasn't any life for a little kid. He was barely seven. He'd been coming here since he was less than a year old. He couldn't remember anything that had happened in his life before. She wrestled a toddler for a truck, and, when she and Bernie had both sat down on the floor, she gave it to her brother. He still liked playing with trucks. The toddler wailed briefly, but soon began to fight another toddler for a car with only three wheels.

"I hate it here," Bernie said, pretending to drive the truck in front of his crossed legs. "I don't know why we have to come all the time."

"'Cause he's our daddy, Bernie. It would just break his heart not to see his family. It's the only thing keeps him going in a place like this. You gotta know someone cares about you, or you just give up."

"Well, I don't care about him," Bernie said, pushing the stupid little truck hard into Angel's shin, daring her to ignore the metal bumper cutting into her flesh. "I hope he just gives up."

"Oh, Bernie, you don't mean that. I know you can't remember. You were only a baby when he left, but he is your daddy. When he comes out . . ." She moved her leg back a little.

"I hope he never comes out," said Bernie, attacking her shin once more.

"Quit it, Bernie. That hurts."

"I know," he said.

She wrenched the truck out of his hand. "If you can't play nice—"

"Go say goodbye to your daddy." Verna was standing above them.

"Is it time already?"

"Way past time. You, too, Bernie. Give him a hug."

Bernie didn't give Wayne a hug, but if saying goodbye meant getting out of there, he was more than glad to obey.

"Bye," he said and bolted for the door.

"Goodbye, Daddy," Angel said. She gave Wayne an awkward hug under the eye of a guard who was making sure she wasn't passing anything to him in the process.

"Bye, angel girl," he said. His face twisted like the face of the little boy she'd scared earlier.

"I'm leaving, Angel."

"Okay, Mama." She tried to smile at Wayne. She didn't want him bawling like a kid in the waiting room. She'd seen other men do that, and it was like watching someone take off all their clothes in public.

"Well, that's that," said Verna when the three of them were back in the truck. "That's the last time you'll ever have to visit this hellhole again."

"Is he coming home?" Angel asked.

"Nope. He *says* they might let him go out on a work crew, but he says a lot of things." Verna started the engine and began to back out of the slot. They were past the outside gates and on the road to the apartment before she spoke again. "Soon as we get to the house, I want you kids to pack up your stuff. We're moving."

"Yippee!" Bernie bounced up and down as high as his seat belt would allow. "Yippee."

"My sentiments exactly," said Verna. "It's well past time for me to put Wayne Morgan behind me and get on with the rest of my life."

"You mean I don't never have to come to jail again?"

"Never," Verna said, patting his bouncing legs.

"Never! Never! Never!" Bernie sang out, throwing both arms in the air like a football player after a touchdown.

If you wish on a star, your wish comes true. Always. Angel felt sick to her stomach.

THREE

"The Bear Went Over the Mountain"

Hurry up, and I mean both of you. I swear, sometimes you kids act like snails on Valium. . . . Get a move on, will you?"

How could Angel hurry? She stared dumbly into the closet. Verna had said she could take only what fit into the green plastic suitcase that Welfare had given her last year so she wouldn't have to carry her stuff around in a garbage bag. She turned to look at the suitcase gaping open on the couch. It seemed to shrink between glances. A garbage bag would have held a lot more stuff. She put her winter jacket into the suitcase. There was hardly any space left. She took the jacket out. Even though it was August, she would have to wear it. She sure wasn't going to leave an almost-new jacket behind. Someone might steal it.

She *had* to take Grizzle. The huge blue plush bear was the last present Daddy had given her before he went to prison. But she couldn't close the lid with Grizzle inside. She'd have to carry him. He was the only one of her animals she cared about. Sweat was breaking out on her forehead as she pulled out both of her drawers and dumped the contents on the couch beside the suitcase.

She should leave behind the clothes she hated and those that she was about to outgrow, even if she still liked them, like the Disney World T-shirt with Goofy on it that Verna had bought at a yard sale. Most of her clothes were getting too small and went back into the drawers.

Underwear. She would have been glad to leave most of that behind, but even if it was holey, she supposed it was necessary. Shoes. She looked at the pairs lolling against each other on the closet floor. Well, she could wear the one pair of sneakers that fit. Her sandals were too worn to bother with, and she hated the red plastic dress-up shoes, which pinched anyhow. Dresses. She had two and she hated them both, but if she didn't have at least one, Verna would be sure to yell at her. Not that they'd be visiting Daddy wherever they were going. Where *were* they going? Maybe to Florida, where it would be warm all the time and all you needed was shorts and T-shirts. Florida. That's where Disney World was. She imagined Verna taking her and Bernie to Disney World. Bernie might be scared of some of those rides, but she wouldn't be. She'd ride everything there, including Space Mountain, which was liable to kill you if you had a weak heart. Hah! It wouldn't bother her a teeny bit.

She put the Disney World T-shirt back in the suitcase. She just might need it. Sweaters. Well, if they were going to Florida, she probably wouldn't need any. Still, Verna hadn't really said anything about Florida. She'd better take a sweater and a sweatshirt. She had a purple one that said BEN AND JERRY'S, which was almost big enough for her, so she stuffed it in. Bernie would like it when she really outgrew it.

Verna stuck her head in the door. "I'm telling you, Angel, quit dreaming and get on with it!" She disappeared across the hall into the bedroom she shared with Bernie.

Even from that distance Angel could hear Bernie whining over everything Verna was packing for him. "Shut up, Bernie. No, you can't take your bed. It belongs with the apartment. There'll be another bed in the new house. Now shut up."

The apartment looked like a hurricane had ripped through it. There was stuff thrown in every direction. Angel stood in the kitchen, waiting for Verna, who was still fighting with Bernie. Now it was over his tricycle. "It's broke, and there won't be no place to ride it anyhow." Was that a clue? There wouldn't be sidewalks where they were going? Maybe a beach. That was it. Florida was nothing but one beach after another. She'd never seen the ocean. A beach, wow! She was roasting in her winter jacket, sweating, and clutching the huge bear and the suitcase. She was afraid to put anything down to open the door for fear Verna would make her leave it behind. Why were they leaving so much behind? Sure, the furniture came with the apartment, but the TV was theirs. She was sure it was, and at least some of the pots and pans. Verna hadn't made any move to pack up the kitchen.

"Are you going to lug that stupid bear?" Verna asked, coming into the kitchen. She was dragging Bernie with one hand and carrying a large brown plastic suitcase in the other.

She put down the suitcase to open the back door. "Leave the suitcases for me. You get your brother and yourself into the truck," she ordered. "I'll be right there." With that, she let go of Bernie's arm and left the kitchen.

Angel was afraid Bernie wouldn't follow her out, but he did. He was whimpering, but he'd given up the fight over his broken tricycle. "I hate her," he said when they got to the truck. "She's mean."

"No," said Angel. "She's just . . ." Just what? She wanted to stick up for their mother. Kids needed to love their moms no matter what, but she didn't know how to say it right. "You heard her, Bernie," she said, opening the passenger door. "Get your butt up into this truck. Now."

She had them both buckled in, Grizzle lying wide-eyed at their feet, when Verna came out of the house. She locked the door behind her, let the screen slam, and threw the suitcases into the back of the pickup. When she climbed into the driver's seat, she looked much less grim than she had all day.

"Okay," she said. "Let's get outta here."

Angel was desperate to ask where they were going, with just two suitcases and an oversized bear for the three of them, but there was something inside her that really didn't want to know the answer.

"Angel won't let me sit by the window," Bernie said as Verna cranked the balky motor.

"Oh, let him have the window, Angel."

"He always puts his hand out. It's dangerous."

"Don't put your hand out, okay, Bernie?"

"Okay," he said.

Angel made the change and buckled them both up again. "Mom, you ought to wear your seat belt."

"Yeah, sure," said Verna. "You're a regular little high-way patrol, aren't you?" But she buckled up. At last the truck motor caught. Verna pressed the gas pedal and made the engine roar a few times before she shifted into reverse and backed out of the driveway. "Say goodbye to Misery Mansion, kids."

"Misery what?" Bernie asked.

"Nothing," said Verna. "Forget it. It's a new day dawning."

"I'm hungry," said Bernie.

"You're always hungry, boy."

"I didn't have no lunch."

"Judas Priest," Verna said. "I never thought about lunch. I'm sorry, old man." She paused at a stop sign and eased her way into traffic. "Soon's we're out of this blinking burg, we'll stop, okay? Just let me get out of here, and we'll stop the first place we see."

"I'm hungry now."

"Shh, Bernie," Angel said. "She said she'd stop soon as she got out of town."

★ ★ ★ ★ ★

Within a few minutes they were on the interstate, the pickup rattling in protest at the speed Verna was demanding from it. They whizzed past an exit that would have taken them into a big shopping area, past some farmland, and then mountains to the left and mountains to the right and trees everywhere. As soon as Bernie realized that there was nothing but trees on either side of the interstate, he started whining again. "I'm hungry. You said we'd stop."

"Well, I will. There just ain't any place to stop right now unless you fancy a maple leaf burger. Would you like that, huh?" Verna leaned across Angel and punched Bernie's arm. "How 'bout a side of tasty French-fried bark, hey?"

"Don't punch me," Bernie ordered grumpily.

"My, my, ain't you the bear. And I thought the bear was riding on the floor."

"He's just hungry," Angel said. She was hungry, too, but Verna was more likely to pay attention to Bernie's belly than to hers.

"Yeah, well, we're all hungry," said Verna. "Soon's we get off the interstate, we can find us a place to eat. Promise."

"You already promised," Bernie said. "You promised soon as we got outta town."

"You *are* a bear, ain't ya? Well, let's sing a song for a bear." She began to sing:

"'The bear went over the mountain,
  The bear went over the mountain,
  The bear went over the mountain,
  To see what he could *eat!*'"

At "eat" she leaned across Angel and made as if to bite Bernie. He shrank back toward the window, but he was trying hard not to smile.

Verna grinned. "Okay," she said, "all together now: 'The bear went over the mountain . . .'" Angel joined in, watching Bernie out of the corner of her eye. They sang the song over and over, always ending with the big bite toward Bernie, until his shadow of a smile broadened and he let out a giggle.

"That's what I like to hear," Verna said. "I like to hear my babies being happy." She sighed. "Not enough laughing in this family. That's for sure. Okay. Now. Let's plan what we're going to eat once we find a place. Me. I think I'll have me a steak about as thick as a brick. How 'bout you, Angel?"

"I don't know. Maybe a hamburger."

"Just a burger? The sky's the limit when you're dreaming, girl. Better dream big."

"Cheeseburger? With fries?"

"That's better. What's Bernie Bear ordering?"

"An elephant."

"Wow. I don't know if we'll have time for an elephant. They take a while to cook."

"A double bacon cheeseburger with giant fries and a milk shake—chocolate," Bernie said.

"I shoulda settled for the elephant. Probably been cheaper."

Bernie giggled again. "But you said—"

"Wow. I gotta be more careful. This mouth of mine is going to get me in trouble big-time!"

Bernie leaned around Angel and growled at Mama. "If you don't watch out, the bear will *eat you up.*"

"Whoa," Verna said. "I'm scared to death."

It was just then, just when they were all having such a great time together, that they heard the noise. "What's that?" Verna leaned out her window.

"It's the pickup," Angel said. Then, through the usual rattle of the truck she heard the *blubbidy blubbidy blubbidy* sound.

"Hell's bells. I got a flat." Verna pulled over to the shoulder and cut off the motor. "And me with no spare."

"You should always have a spare, Mama. It's not safe not to—"

"Give me a break, Angel. I don't always do what I ought to, okay? Satisfied?" Verna climbed out and walked around the truck.

"I want to see!" Bernie said, reaching for his seat belt.

Angel grabbed his hand. "We better stay here," she said. "It'll just make her madder if we get out."

They watched anxiously as Verna lifted the hood and then walked several yards ahead and began to wave at passing cars. It was ages before anyone stopped. When at last a guy in a pickup older than their own pulled over, Verna ran up to his window. They talked for a few minutes, and then the pickup drove off. Verna came back and climbed into the cab.

"Why wouldn't he help us, Mama?" Bernie asked.

Verna sighed. "I haven't got a spare. He's got to send somebody back who can tow us to a station. "That's all I need today. A tow charge *and* a new tire." She put her head down on the steering wheel. "Oh Lord, can't anything ever go right? What did I ever do?"

Angel wanted to comfort her. She wanted to put her hand on Verna's back and tell her everything was going to be all right, but she wasn't sure it would be.

It seemed like hours before the tow truck came. The driver didn't want all three of them squeezing into his cab, and for a minute Angel was afraid Verna might leave them behind. But she took Bernie on her lap and sweet-talked the guy into taking them all along. It was hours more at the station while the man sent to somewhere else to get the right-sized tire. When it looked as though everything was taken care of and they were all set to go, the guy told Verna her credit card was maxed out. Verna said that was not possible and the guy said it was, too, and how was she going to pay for the tire and the tow? Verna started cussing him out, right there in front of everybody, and the man got red in the face and started cussing back.

Angel tried her best to keep Bernie out of the way, but before she could stop him, he was grabbing Verna's shirt right in the middle of the fight. "Mama, I need some chips!"

Verna turned, scowling. "Just get in the damn truck, Bernie. You, too, Angel. I'll work this out. I know somebody I can call. You two just get in the truck and don't give me any more grief, you hear?"

★ ★ ★ ★ ★

"I just wanted something to eat." Bernie's lip was stuck out almost as far as the windshield.

"I know, Bernie, but she's trying to work things out. We can't interrupt."

They strained their necks, looking in all directions, for whoever might be coming to their rescue. At last, a rusty Subaru wagon drove up, and a man Angel had never seen before got out, but he must have been the one Verna was waiting for because she came running out of the station and threw her arms around him. Then she stuck her arm through his and led him inside.

"Why was Mama hugging that man?" Bernie asked.

"She's just thanking him for coming to help her," Angel said. "It doesn't mean anything."

It *couldn't* mean anything. Verna was married. Married people didn't go around hugging people who weren't their husbands. She thought Verna would bring their rescuer over and introduce him, but when the man came out, he said a few words to Verna and then, with only a quick glance at the pickup and the two children peering out the window, went back to his car and drove away.

At least, Angel thought, Verna would explain who the man was. But all she said was, "Well, that's it. We can get going now."

Bernie slumped against the door. He was tired, Angel saw. She gave a big yawn. Bernie yawned in echo. "How 'bout Bernie and me take a nap, Mom?"

"I'm not tired," Bernie said, trying to cover another yawn. "I'm hungry."

"Well, it won't hurt you to be quiet and give Angel and me both some rest."

Angel closed her eyes and tilted her head back against the seat. Verna switched on the radio. "Find me a station, Angel," she said.

Angel wound the dial past all the noisy rock stations until she found one that was playing a gentle music that wrapped its arms around her. It reminded her of a field trip last year to hear the Vermont Symphony. All the kids had really liked the concert, but they pretended they'd been bored. Only stuck-up rich people were supposed to like that kind of music. Angel relaxed into the sound. Soon she heard Bernie's gentle snore.

Angel hadn't meant to sleep. She'd just meant to make Bernie take a nap, but it had been a hard day, and before she knew it Verna was slowing the car. Angel sat up abruptly. They were at a traffic light.

"Well, sleeping beauty, awake, without a kiss."

"I was just resting my eyes."

"Said the potato."

Angel made herself giggle. When Verna made a joke, she liked people to laugh.

"I have a feeling," Verna said, "there's a fast-food heaven around here somewhere."

She turned left, and, sure enough, within a mile or so they came upon the familiar herd of arches, huts, buckets of chicken, and burger joints. Verna pulled into the first one and hopped out, yelling as she did so, "C'mon, kids. Time to eat."

"Bernie's still asleep, Mama."

"Just leave him in the truck, then. We'll bring something out."

"You can't do that!" Honestly, sometimes she felt older than Verna. Everybody knew you couldn't leave a little kid unattended in a vehicle.

"Well, you wake him up. I'll be inside." She slammed the driver-side door and marched into the restaurant, leaving two kids unattended in a vehicle. Verna's mood changed faster than Vermont weather.

"Wake up, Bernie!" Angel shook his arm. "We're at McDonald's."

Bernie was not about to wake up. Angel shook him harder and yelled and threatened. Finally, he opened his eyes partway. "Shuddup," he said grumpily.

"You want Mama and me just to leave you out here while we eat?" Unbuckling both their seat belts, she reached across him and opened the door. "Get out, Bernie."

"Umm," he muttered.

She climbed over him to the running board and began yanking at his arm. "Get out this minute, Bernie Elvis Morgan, or I'm telling you, you'll be sorry. Mama's so mad she might just leave you here forever." The lie worked. Bernie's eyes fluttered open. He grunted and climbed out of the pickup. She pushed down the lock, slammed the door, and, with Bernie stumbling after her, went inside.

For a moment, she didn't see Verna. Maybe she *had* left them. No, there she was in a booth. Angel dragged Bernie over. "I got you kids Happy Meals," Verna said. She didn't seem too happy about it.

When he heard "Happy Meals," Bernie came wide awake. "I don't want a Happy Meal."

"Well, they was clean out of elephants. Sit down and eat." It was the tone of voice that even Bernie obeyed.

"You get a toy in a Happy Meal," Angel whispered.

Bernie scowled.

"You can have mine, too."

"And your fries?"

Angel handed over the toy, then the fries, without watching. She was looking at her mother, who had not ordered a steak. They didn't have them at McDonald's, did they? Mama had nothing in front of her worn-out face but a cup of coffee about a foot high. She was barely sipping at it.

"You okay, Mama?"

"Yeah, sure. Why wouldn't I be? I got a husband in jail and two kids around my neck and I'm heading right back to—Bernie Elvis Morgan! Can't you do nothing right?" Verna slid to the left and jumped to her feet in one quick motion. Bernie had knocked his soda over, and it was pouring across the tabletop right toward where her lap had been. Angel ran for napkins and came back with a handful. Bernie's face was scrunched up, ready to bawl.

"Don't cry, Bernie," Angel begged as she tried desperately to sop up the sticky liquid. "You can have mine."

"I'll see you kids in the truck." Verna snatched her purse off the table and stomped out.

"Get up, Bernie." Angel was frantic. "Here, take your Happy Meal. You can eat in the truck." She dropped the sopping napkins on the table, grabbed what was left of her burger in one hand and her mother's coffee in the other, and, half pushing Bernie ahead of her, hurried to the truck. It was still there. She went around to the driver's side. "I brought your coffee, Mama."

Verna rolled down her window and took the Styrofoam cup, nodding a begrudging thanks. She was furious. "He didn't mean to, Mama," Angel said. "He was tired and sleepy. It was my fault. I made him come in."

"I swear, I don't know what I'm going to do with you kids."

"We'll be good, Mama. Could you—could you please unlock the other door?"

"Oh, for pity sake, Angel." She stretched over and pulled up the button.

Bernie was standing crying beside the truck, his fries in one hand and the action figures and his half-eaten burger clutched together in the other. Angel reached up and opened the door for him. "You want to sit by Mama or you want the window?" she asked quietly.

"Window." He mouthed the word.

The Other Side of the Mountain

Verna juggled the coffee, changed gears, and steered, all at the same time. Couldn't she see how dangerous that was? Besides, she hadn't fastened her seat belt.

"Want me to hold your coffee?"

"Huh? No. I can manage."

Angel opened her mouth to object, but closed it again without saying anything. She took a bite of her burger and chewed. Something the size of a golf ball was blocking her throat, and it was hard to swallow. "Eat, Bernie," she commanded out of the side of her mouth.

"She promised me a double bacon cheeseburger and a chocolate milk shake," he muttered.

"She was just pretending, Bernie."

"Well, I wudn't pretending."

"Better just eat what you got."

"Where's my soda?"

"You spilled it, remember?"

"You said I could have yours."

"I couldn't carry it, Bernie. I had my hands full."

"I need something to drink." His voice was louder now. Verna was sure to hear him whining.

"Shh, Bernie, please. I can't help it. Just eat what you got. Mama'll get you a drink next time we stop."

"And when is that going to be? Never. Never. Never. Never."

"Shut up whining, Bernie. I'm trying to drive," Verna said.

"See, Bernie, you're bothering Mama."

"I don't care. I want a milk shake and I want it now. Right this minute."

Verna jerked the pickup over and slammed on the brakes. "I've had enough of your whining, Bernie Elvis. Now you shut up or get out of this truck and walk."

"Mama!" Angel cried. "She doesn't mean it, Bernie."

"The hell I don't. Now, are you going to shut up and eat your food or what?"

"Shuddup and eat my food," said Bernie, his voice tiny and trembly. Verna shouldn't scare him like that. He was only a little kid.

"That's better." Verna pulled out into the road again. "I don't mean to be ugly to you kids, but I got my limits. Understand?"

"Yes." Both children whispered the word. Bernie looked like he was going to cry, so Angel handed him the rest of her hamburger.

★   ★   ★   ★   ★

They were leaving the town now and heading out into real country. The road was two narrow lanes with lots of hills and curves with pastures and woods on either side.

There wouldn't be any place to buy a milk shake. Angel felt pretty sure about that. Cows looked up as they passed, chewing idly and staring after the car like nosy neighbors. Angel leaned across Bernie and stuck her tongue out at one of them. The cow tossed her head and walked away.

Bernie's pinched face relaxed. He turned and stuck his tongue out at the disappearing black-and-white forms. Watching the rear ends waddle away, tails switching, they both giggled.

"Well, I'm glad somebody's happy for a change," Verna said, speeding through a tiny village. Angel opened her mouth to suggest they stop at the general store that she could see from the crossroad, but Verna was intent on the road ahead. The village was far behind them before Angel could even try to get the words out.

"Won't be long now, kids, promise." Angel had long ago learned not to rely on Verna's promises, so it was no surprise when Verna did a tight U-turn in the middle of the narrow road and started back in the direction of the village. She cursed under her breath.

"Are we lost?" Bernie asked.

"No, Mr. Smarty-pants, we are not lost. Just somebody thought it would be cute to take down the blinking road sign."

"Don't you know the way?" His voice was high and pinched.

"Of course I know the way. It's just been a while since

I been here, and everything looks different." She made a quick cut onto a dirt road. "Relax. This is it."

But it wasn't. Neither were the next three dirt roads they tried, although Verna kept assuring them that she had found the right road, but each one either petered out into a dead end or came to a crossroad that proved her wrong.

"It'll be dark soon. Maybe we should ask directions—" Angel began.

Verna snapped her off. "And just who from, Miss Know-it-all? You see anybody I can ask directions from?"

"We could go back to . . ."

"Not on your sweet life. I'm through going back." In the end, however, they did go back down the paved road, not, as Angel had hoped, to the village with the general store, where they could have gotten Bernie a drink, but to a lonely old house somewhere along the way. The paint was peeling, and the roof of the attached barn was half caved in. Verna jumped out of the truck, leaving the motor running. This time Angel didn't protest.

"I got to pee."

"Can't you wait, Bernie?" Angel eyed the house. She didn't think Verna would be too happy if they appeared beside her at the door asking to use the toilet.

"No. I can't wait. That's all anybody ever says to me. Wait. Wait. Wait. Well, I can't wait."

She leaned over and unbuckled his belt. "Okay. Okay, hop out and go behind the truck. You don't want anybody to see you."

"They'll see me from the road."

"Do you see anybody coming or going on that road? C'mon, Bernie. If you gotta go, go, and be quick about it." She unlatched the door. Bernie climbed out. "And pull your pants down. You don't want to wet them."

Verna came out of the house and jumped into the cab. "Okay," she said. "All set."

"Mama! Wait for Bernie!"

Verna looked over toward the open door of the cab. "Where the hell?"

"He's just going to pee." She leaned out. "Hurry, Bernie. Mama's ready to go."

"Wait! Mama, wait! I'm coming right now!" Bernie scrambled awkwardly into the truck, trying to pull his pants up as he came.

"You just better hurry," Verna said, throwing the truck into gear and starting into the road. "Before those folks catch you peeing in their yard."

Bernie tried desperately to pull the door shut after him, but it wouldn't close. Angel leaned across him and grabbed the handle. "Mama, slow down. Please. The door's not shut, and Bernie's not buckled in either."

Verna stopped the truck with a jerk. She sat there, her hands drumming on the steering wheel, while Angel first helped Bernie get his pants up all the way to his belly button, buckled his seat belt, and then yanked the door shut hard. At the sound, Verna turned to look at her. "You're quite the little mother, Angel." Angel wasn't

sure whether it was a compliment or not, so she just
nodded.

They drove past the place on the road where Verna
had made the U-turn, a long way past, so that Angel was
afraid they would be lost again, but Verna was slowing
the car at every corner, looking for signs. She must have
spotted the missing sign she'd been looking for, because
now they were turning right onto a dirt road she hadn't
tried earlier.

In the gathering dusk Angel could just make out the
white lettering. "Morgan Farm Road! That's our name."

"Your daddy's people's name. Yeah."

"Did you see that sign, Bernie? This road has our name
on it!" Bernie just looked at her. He was still mad at Mama,
breaking her promises and almost leaving him behind at
least twice, but Angel couldn't help being excited. Morgan
Farm Road. It was hard to imagine relatives so important
that a whole road would be named after them. That was
like Washington Street or Ethan Allen Boulevard. She
wanted to ask Mama if they were going to the actual
Morgan Farm that the road was named after, but Verna
was leaning out of the window, looking for a left-hand
turn. Better not to bother her with questions right now.

"Okay, this is it," Verna said.

The mailbox with MORGAN in faded blue paint was
almost hidden by bushes. You'd wonder how the mail-
man would get to it and put mail in it. Angel's tummy
began to tighten up. She wanted to grab Bernie's hand,

but she grabbed her own instead. This was the place, she knew it. Their new home. The dirt driveway was shorter than the one in Burlington. Almost at once they were sitting in front of a house that—was it possible?—that Angel knew she had seen before.

"Have I ever been here?" she asked.

"Both you kids been here, but Bernie wouldn't remember. You ought to, though."

"Yeah," said Angel. This was where that trailer was. She was sure of it. Instinctively, she looked to the right. Yes, on the other side of the junk-filled front yard, just beyond what was left of the fence, there was the trailer, paint peeling, with weeds all around its base, but there it was. The house didn't look in much better condition than the trailer. It had been white once, or gray. It wasn't much of anything now but bare wood. There were panes broken in several of the windows. Someone had taped newspaper to cover the holes.

"It looks like a haunted house," said Bernie, and it did look spooky in the twilight.

"Okay, kids. Wait here a minute. I'll be right back, but first I got to talk to Grandma." Verna jumped out of the cab but slowed as she climbed the steps to the porch and approached the door. Angel could see her, her fist in the air, just holding it back, as though trying to get up the nerve to knock. *I bet she didn't even say we were coming. I bet this Grandma person doesn't even know we're coming to live with her.*

"I don't want to live here, Angel." Bernie had jammed himself against her, and although Verna had by now disappeared behind the shabby door, he was whispering, "I don't like it here."

"It'll be okay, Bernie," she said, and as she said the words, she almost believed them herself, because she found herself remembering something. She couldn't have said what it was. It was more like a smell you recognize but can't name. Something good had happened to her here. In all the craziness before Wayne went to jail, something good had happened here.

It seemed ages before the door opened and Verna came out alone to the car. Angel was already steeling herself for a trip back to the city, but instead Verna said, "Okay. We can stay, but you kids gotta be quiet as bunny rabbits. Your great-grandma is an old lady. She won't tolerate any of your screaming and carrying on."

"I don't want to stay here," Bernie said. His voice was quiet but stubborn. "I want to go home."

Verna ignored him. She was getting the suitcases out of the back and waving with her head for the children to follow her. Angel unbuckled them both and nudged her brother. "Don't worry, Bernie. I'll be here with you. Haven't I always taken care of you?"

"I don't wanta . . ." he started, then bit his lip and clambered down out of the cab.

Angel pulled Grizzle off the floor. "Here," she said. "You want to hold on to Grizzle? Just for a little while? I can't give him to you. It would hurt Daddy's feelings if I gave him away, but you can sleep with him for a while if you want to."

He grabbed Grizzle's fat neck and buried his face in the blue plush. Angel took his free hand, and together they walked up the rickety steps, across the porch crammed so full of junk that there was only a narrow path to the door. "Stand up straight, Bernie." She took a deep breath and stood up straighter herself. "We got to make a good impression."

Hansel and Grizzle

They stepped through the front door into a hall. Ahead of them was a dark staircase, on one side a closed door, on the other an open one. "In here," Verna called. They followed her voice to the open door. At first, neither of them saw the old lady. Although it was still twilight outside, the house was as dark as night. Angel blinked and looked around. It seemed to be a kitchen. The room was hot and stuffy, as though no one ever opened the windows. If they walked straight in they would walk into a table, so she stood still in the doorway, holding Bernie's hand, waiting for Verna to tell them what to do. It was too easy to start off wrong in a strange situation. She wanted to warn Bernie not to whine or ask for a milk shake, but she didn't dare speak out loud.

"Who's that, Angel?" See? She should have told Bernie to keep quiet, and now it was too late. Up until then his left arm had been squeezed around Grizzle's neck in a death grip and his right hand tight in Angel's hand, but he dropped the bear on the floor and let go of Angel's hand at the same time. His curiosity had overcome his fear. "Angel, I said, 'Who's that?'" He pointed at something beyond the left side of the table.

"Shh, Bernie. And don't point. It's not polite." Angel grabbed his outstretched finger, but he wrenched free and headed around the table for a closer look.

"So these are the kids, huh?" The voice was coming from a rocker tucked between a huge black woodstove, which didn't seem to be lit, and a long, rough wooden counter with cabinets above and below and a sink three-quarters of the way to the opposite wall. The person in the rocker seemed to be bundled up in blankets. "Wouldn't of known them."

"Well, you can't really see them now, can you, Grandma?" Verna said. Her voice was fakey cheerful. "Don't you ever pull up the shades?"

The old woman shook her head. "You leave my shades be, Verna."

"Well, just let me turn on a light, okay? They're pretty cute kids, if I do say so myself." There was a bare light-bulb hanging not quite over the center of the table. Verna fiddled with the wall switch and got a faint glow from the dusty bulb. "You behave yourself now, Bernie," she said through gritted teeth.

By this time Bernie was standing squarely in front of the rocker. "Are you cold?" he asked.

"I'm always cold," the old woman snapped. "That's what happens to you when you get old like me. You ain't never warm. Not even in the summer."

"Oh. Then why don't you turn on your furnace?"

"Because I ain't got one."

"You got a stove. Why don't you turn that on?"

"Bernie," Verna said. "Don't you go asking your great-grandma a lot of questions."

He ignored her. "I'm hungry," he said to the old woman.

"Bernie!" Angel said.

"That's enough, Bernie." Any fake cheer had left Verna's voice. "I'm warning you."

"Well, I wasn't exactly expecting company," the old woman said, sliding her eyes toward Verna. "I don't know what there is to eat around here."

Bernie glanced back at Verna to see how close she was to him before he leaned over and said something into the old woman's ear.

She began to laugh, a funny laugh, like her laugh box had rusted and she couldn't make it work smoothly. "Pizza!" she said, almost choking on the words. "Now, where in the blazes am I going to find a pizza around here?"

"Angel. Take your brother upstairs this minute." Then, as if realizing that she hadn't really cleared anything with the old woman, she changed to her sweet tone of voice, "Which room do you want the kids in, Grandma?"

"I don't guess it matters none. Either room. They ain't neither of them clean. I wasn't exactly expecting—"

"Take your brother up," Verna ordered. "I'll be right there."

Bernie still hung around the old woman's chair, so there was nothing for Angel to do but go around the table and grab his hand. "C'mon, Bernie."

"So this is Angel." The old woman stretched out a bony finger as though to touch her.

Angel shrank back a little. She didn't mean to, but she couldn't help it. There was a funny stale smell coming from the bundle of blankets in the rocker.

"I won't bite you, girl." Angel turned to look straight in the woman's face. Was that what the witch had said to Hansel and Gretel? A black mole with a stiff wire of white hair coming out of it grew almost on the tip of the old woman's nose. Just like a witch, except . . .

"You remember me?" She peered up into Angel's face. There was a little spit in the corner of her mouth.

Angel started to shake her head, but something stopped her. "I used to—to play with your nose," she said.

The woman cackled her rusty laugh. "That's right, you did. I forgot that."

"It's funny looking," Bernie said. He reached out to finger it. Angel grabbed his hand.

"Don't, Bernie. That's not polite."

The strange laugh again. "You got mighty polite in your old age, Miss Angel."

"I said, Take your brother upstairs," Verna said. "Grandma and I got stuff to talk about."

"There ain't any sheets on the beds. I wasn't expecting—"

"Git!"

This time Verna meant business. Both children headed for the door. Angel grabbed up Grizzle and pushed Bernie ahead of her out into the hall and up the dark, narrow wooden stairs. Partway up he stumbled, but she caught him before they both fell backward.

"Stop pushing, Angel."

"I'm not pushing. Just get going before Mama yells again, okay?"

"I'm going as fast as I can. If I fall down and break my head, it will be all your fault—"

"I said hurry."

"—and you'll be sorry sorry sorry." They were at the top by the time he finished his string of sorrys.

"Did Mama say right or left?" Angel asked, anxious. She felt as though she and Bernie had too many wrong things going against them already. She needed to get something right.

"I'm not going to tell you."

Peering into the darkness, she poked her head first into one room and then the other. In the room on the right, she thought she could make out two small beds. "I think this one's ours, Bernie." She turned just in time to see Bernie starting back down the stairs. She grabbed him by the arm. "No, you don't!"

"I'm hungry," he said, trying to yank away.

"So am I, but there's nothing I can do about it, is there, until Mama says so, so just come on in here and sit down and behave yourself for once in your life." She dragged him into the room on the right side of the hall.

"You hurt my arm."

"Well, I can't trust you one minute, Bernie. The second I let go you're— Okay, okay." His face was screwed up ready to yell. "Okay, don't cry. I'll let go if you promise not to run back downstairs until Mama says so. Okay?"

He nodded.

She plopped him down on the nearest bed and shoved Grizzle at him. Automatically, he clutched the bear in his left arm and stuck his right thumb in his mouth. He'd probably be sucking his thumb after he could shave.

"Now, you sit right there, and I'll find a light switch so we won't have to sit up here in the dark, okay?" There was no switch evident in the dim light of the room, but there was a bare bulb hanging down from the ceiling, so there had to be some way to turn it on. She felt all around the wall. Behind her back a light went on.

Bernie was standing on the bed under the bulb, grinning.

"Where was the switch?"

"I yanked the string and it came on," he said, as proud as if he'd just invented electricity.

"Okay, but you shouldn't fool with it."

"I just pulled the string. I didn't fool with it. See?" He pulled the string off and on to show her.

"Don't!"

"Why not?" He pulled it again. "I was just showing you."

"Okay, you showed me. Now, sit down and behave yourself."

"Why don't you sit down yourself, Miss Boss?"

She sat down beside him. Grizzle lay on the floor between the two beds where Bernie had dropped him in the excitement over the stupid lightbulb. She reached for the bear and dusted him off. For a few seconds she held him, rubbing her cheek against his ear.

Bernie was staring at her. "What's the matter, Angel?"

"Nothing." She gave the bear a pat and put it down beside her on the bed, which was covered with a worn quilt, torn along most of its patches. Pulling off her sweaty jacket, she laid it on the bed beyond Grizzle. She'd have to find out where to put their stuff, but that would have to wait. Now she sat as still as she could, trying in vain to make the murmur of voices from the kitchen below into words. Bernie was quiet, too. Too quiet. She turned to see him neatly picking at a loose patch on the quilt. He had it free on three sides before she caught him.

"Don't!" she cried. "You'll tear it up!"

"It's already tore up."

"Not so bad as it will be if you keep monkeying with it." She patted at his hand to make him stop.

"Quit it! You're always hitting me. Always. Always. Always."

"I never hit you, Bernie, you know that. Here." She handed him Grizzle. "Want a story?"

"What kind of story?" He stuck his thumb in his mouth and began picking at the blue plush on the bear.

She wanted to tell him not to, that Grizzle was her bear, not his to pick bald, but she controlled herself. *A story.* The only story she could think of at the moment was Hansel and Grizzle; no, Gretel. Hansel and Gretel.

"Once upon a time," she began, remembering as she went along that the evil mother made the father take the children deep into the woods, where they met a witch. She prayed her mother would call up the stairs and interrupt. Soon.

"So the children had to spend the night in the woods."

Bernie pulled his thumb out of his mouth. "Were they scared?"

"Well, sure, but Hansel was very brave."

"That was the brother, right?"

"The *big* brother. He didn't suck his thumb. He was too brave, and besides, all these angels came and watched over them so none of the wild animals could eat them up."

"I'm hungry."

She hurried on. "In the morning they began to try to find their way home."

"I want to go home, Angel. I don't like it here."

"We hardly got here, Bernie. You might like it after a while. When you're used to it."

"I won't never get used to it. Never. Never. Never."

"You're always saying 'never,' Bernie. How do you know? This might be the best place we've ever lived."

"It'll be the worst. I know." He got up and went over to the small window in the eaves. He was quiet for a while. Then she could see his little body tensing up. "Angel," he whispered. "There's a robber out there."

"Oh, Bernie, you know there's not!"

"Come here and see if you don't believe me."

She got up and went over to the window. "Where?" she asked.

He pointed to the left. There was a dark figure moving toward the corner of the house. "See? I told you," he said. "Now do you believe me?"

She put her arm around his shoulders. They were both shivering.

Santy Claus

You better call the police," said Bernie.

A picture flashed through Angel's head. It was night. Angel was suddenly awake, her heart pounding. *Bang Bang Bang.* Someone was banging on the front door. *Police! Open up!* When no one opened the door that night, they crashed it in and took Daddy away. "No," she said, "not the police, Bernie."

"You got to. See that gun?" The figure had something in his hands, something huge, like the biggest gun Angel had ever seen outside a war movie on TV. A bazooka—that's what they called them.

"Angel. What if he's coming to kill us dead?"

She tightened her grip around his shoulders. "Of course he's not, silly." She couldn't stand to see him so afraid. "It's nothing, I'm sure. But if you like, I'll just go down and tell Mama, okay?"

"Don't leave me up here by myself!"

"Okay, but you got to be quiet. Let me do the talking. Promise?"

"Yeah, I promise." He didn't object when she took his hand.

As they sidled down the narrow staircase, the voices from the kitchen grew louder. Verna's voice came through clearly. "Just for a few days, I swear," she was saying. "No more than a week."

Angel froze on the next-to-bottom step. She strained to make out the words of the reply, but they were muffled and impossible to understand.

"I got a little cash," Verna said next. "Enough to cover food for the week."

What does Verna mean about a week? She told us this was our new home.

Mumble. Mumble.

"Well, I can't be responsible for Wayne. You raised him. I didn't." Verna's voice was shrill as a crow squawk.

Bernie punched Angel in the ribs. "Go on, Angel. You got to tell her."

"I can't, Bernie. I think they're having a fi—important discussion."

"Then I'll tell her."

She tried to stop him, but he was too quick for her. He jerked loose, darted around her, and raced into the kitchen, waving his arms. "Mama! Mama!" he cried. "There's a man out there with a big gun and he's going to kill us all dead!"

Verna spun around, her mouth still open for whatever she had planned to say next, obviously furious at being interrupted. "What's the matter with you, Bernie? What are you doing down here?" She looked over his head to

Angel, still standing in the doorway. "What do you mean coming down here when I told you to stay upstairs?"

"I told you already, Mama," Bernie cried. "There's a man out there with a big gun!"

"I never heard such fool talk in my life. Get back up those stairs this minute!"

Bernie made a dash for the rocker. "She won't never believe me," he said to the old woman. "I did see him. I did. I did."

Grandma stuck a hand out of the blankets and put it on Bernie's head. "Calm down, boy. That was probably just Santy Claus out there with some big old toy."

"Santa Claus? Really?" Bernie turned to look at Angel, his eyes sparkling in the dim light. For a minute he was caught up in the idea, but then he turned back to the rocker. "How could it be Santa Claus? It ain't even Christmas."

"You never know about old Santy Claus. Maybe he's just scouting you out—seeing where you got yourself off to. He's got to keep track of all the kiddies, you know."

"Yeah. He's got to know where I moved to, right?"

"You got it, boy."

"I guess he'd be mad if he knew we was spying on him."

"You got that right. Santy Claus is like some of the rest of us." She turned to look at Verna. "He don't want nobody poking into his private business."

Angel didn't know what to do. The old woman was as crazy as Bernie. "He really did see someone, Mama," she said.

"I don't care what he thinks he saw. I want you kids to stop your nonsense and get up those stairs before I take a belt—"

"I'm hungry." Bernie was leaning against the rocker, looking into the old face, his voice sweet as pure maple syrup.

"Don't you ever feed these children, Verna?"

"'Course I feed them."

"Not supper," Bernie said. "And I still ain't had my milk shake."

The old woman slowly unwrapped her blankets and began to hoist herself out of the chair, looking as though she might just snap into pieces from the effort. "I don't know what I got. I wasn't expecting—"

Verna gave another of her fake laughs. "Oh, Grandma, forget it. He always says he's hungry. It don't mean nothing. He's just trying to get attention." She glared at Bernie, daring him to contradict her. But Bernie wasn't paying any attention. He was staring at the old woman, who was lifting her body bone by bone from the rocker.

"Angel and me can help, can't we, Angel?" he said anxiously.

Angel's eyes darted back and forth between Verna and Grandma. She didn't know how to answer. Bernie, meantime, had taken Grandma's hand and was leading her over to the refrigerator. It was small and square and had coils on the top, as ancient as its owner. The old woman opened the door. No light came on. She stuck in her head. Bernie shoved his small one in beside hers.

"Not much in there," he said. "But you wasn't expecting us, was you?"

"If someone would have give me a call, I could have sent to the store," Grandma said.

"Oh, I'll go to the store," Verna said impatiently.

"No, you won't."

Verna opened her mouth to argue.

"It's closed." Grandma took a dish out of the fridge and shut the door. "Angel, whyn't you look in that cabinet over there? See if they's beans or anything."

"I don't like beans," Bernie said.

"I thought you said you was hungry. If you ain't hungry, no sense bothering."

Angel shook her head toward Bernie before going to the cabinet and opening the door. There were two shelves packed with cans. Cans of pork and beans crowding each other like people pushing to be first in a store sale. Toward the end of the top shelf, the beans turned into peaches. She took out a can of beans. "Want me to heat this up?" she asked, keeping an eye on Verna, who was still puffy with anger.

"That'd be nice. The hot plate is down this ways." She waved a hand at it. "I don't want to light the stove for a can of beans. Waste of good firewood."

"You still cooking on the woodstove, Grandma? I can't believe it."

"Some of us ain't got the money to go out and buy us a fancy propane range."

Angel stood by the counter with the can in her hand. Should she rummage around in the drawers and cabinets to find a can opener and a saucepan, or should she ask?

"The drawer by the sink, girl, if you're looking for the opener. Bernie, get down on your knees and find your sister a pan. No, not that door—the next one. That's it. Yeah, that one will do."

The can opener was not like the one on the wall at the apartment. While she was still trying to figure it out, Verna came over and took the can and the opener out of her hands. "I'll do it." She sighed. "Can you believe this woman?" she muttered. "Here." She handed Angel the opened can, the jagged lid still hanging on by a narrow spit of metal.

Angel poured the beans into the pot and switched on the hot plate. "Spoon?" she asked the old woman quietly, trying not to get Verna more upset.

"That drawer in front of your belly has the spoons," Grandma said.

Angel nodded and tried to smile a thank-you before she turned her full attention to heating the beans, stirring them constantly with the old pitted metal spoon. She was terrified she might let them burn and cause even more unhappiness.

Neither Verna nor Grandma ate any beans. At first, Bernie just ate the dish of peaches Grandma had gotten out of the fridge, but after Angel kicked him, he took a bite of beans, squirreling them in his cheeks as he always did with food he didn't like.

"Chew," Angel commanded under her breath.

"They'll probably poison me," he muttered back.

"Chew, Bernie, or else!" She repeated, keeping her voice too low for the women to hear. Grandma had eased her body back down in the rocker, wrapped herself in the blankets, and was rocking away with her eyes half shut. Verna was pacing around, opening cabinet doors and drawers and humphing and grunting.

"Okay," she said suddenly. "Bedtime! Up you go!"

"Bernie hasn't eaten his beans yet."

"Well, he's had plenty of time to. I don't think Mr. Bernie was as hungry as he let on to be."

"I wanted a milk shake."

"Well, I wanted to win the Tri-State Lottery. Go on. I'll get the bags. I said go on. Angel, take your brother upstairs. Now!"

Angel jumped to her feet. "C'mon, Bernie. You heard Mama."

His eyes were hard as little BB gun pellets, but he got up and followed Angel up the stairs, stamping his feet on every step to let Verna know what he was thinking of her.

"Stop it, Bernie. You'll upset your great-grandma. We promised to be nice so she'd let us live here."

"Was that *really* Santa Claus out there?" he asked.

"Of course not. Don't be silly."

"Then I don't want to live here."

"I don't think we get to choose, Bernie. I think it's all decided."

Before long, Verna appeared at the door with sheets in her arms. "Angel, help Bernie get on his PJs. The bathroom is off the kitchen, so you better go now and get it over with for the night." Bernie was sitting on the side of his bed with his back to her. "What's the matter, Bernie?"

He didn't answer. She walked around and sat down beside him. "I said . . ." Her voice was suddenly gentle. "I said, What's the matter?" She brushed the hair out of his face.

"I don't like it here," he said. "There ain't no Santa Claus and I hate beans. I want to go home."

"You're just going to have to be brave, okay? You'll get used to it. You'll like the country. There's lots to do in the country."

"What?"

"Well . . ." she paused as though trying hard to think of something. "Well, you can play outside all you want. There's no traffic or strangers or—"

"There is, too, strangers. We saw him out the window."

She made a high-pitched sound like a TV laugh track. "You got the best imagination. I swear."

"That Grandma woman lied. She said it was Santa Claus."

"Well, maybe it was Santa Claus. I been wrong before, God knows." She leaned over and kissed him on the forehead. "You be a big brave man for Mama, hear? And stay out of trouble, okay?" She stood up abruptly, her I-mean-business self again. "All right now, Bernie, hop off the bed. Here, Angel, give me a hand with these sheets."

Bernie dragged Grizzle off the bed by one ear and stood against the wall, sucking his thumb and fingering the bear's ear while Angel and Mama made both beds.

"Okay," Verna said, straightening up. "Pajamas, bathroom, bed. And make it quick!" By the time she finished the order they could hear her heels clicking on the stairs.

Angel's clothes were folded neatly in her suitcase, so she found her pajamas at once. She was ready to go down while Bernie was still churning stuff around in the big brown case. "Stop that, Bernie! You'll mess everything up."

"No, I won't," Bernie said. "It's my stuff and I can mess it up all I want to. Here they are. See? You didn't think I could find them and I did. So there."

They crept down the stairs.

Verna was sitting in a kitchen chair, smoking a cigarette. Grandma was still rocking. Didn't she ever do anything else? "We got to go to the bathroom," Angel said.

"Well, hurry," Verna said.

"Mama, I forgot me and Bernie's toothbrushes."

"Didn't I tell you to check the bathroom? Sheesh. Can't you remember nothing? You're eleven years old, Angel. You got to be responsible."

"I'm sorry."

"Well, go on. Get through in the bathroom. We'll worry about toothbrushes later."

★ ★ ★ ★ ★

Something woke her up. It was pitch dark with no streetlight to shine through the window. There was the sound of a car. No—the sound of a balky pickup engine starting. Angel sat up in bed. Suddenly, she realized that the clothes in the big suitcase were all Bernie's. Verna hadn't brought any of her own clothes. She listened until the noise of the motor died away in the distance.

SEVEN

Star Man

Angel tried to tell herself that Verna had just gone to run an errand. That was it. She'd gone to get some Sugar Pops. Bernie loved Sugar Pops. Wouldn't Verna want him to have something special, since he never got his milk shake and supper was only canned peaches and beans, which he hated? It would take her a long time to find a store that was still open. She might have to go all the way to a big town like the one where they had all the fast-food places. Little towns wouldn't have supermarkets that stayed open all night. Angel ought to get some sleep. It would be an hour or so before Verna could get back. No reason to just lie here and worry.

She didn't bring any clothes. Of course Verna had brought clothes. They were just in another suitcase, not mixed up with Bernie's. Why would she pack her things with Bernie's? She'd want to keep them neat and— Well, Angel hadn't actually seen another suitcase, but that didn't mean there wasn't one. There'd been plenty of time for Verna to pack one and put it in the back of the pick-up when Angel was busy packing or seeing to Bernie.

How come she left the pots and pans behind? How come she didn't bring the almost-new TV?

Angel flung herself over and yanked the quilt up to her neck. Even though it was summer and the room was hot, she felt cold. It was one thing to leave your kids in an all-night diner by mistake. It was something else to leave them in the country on purpose. That would be too much like Hansel and Gretel. *She's gone back to pack everything up and clear out of the apartment. She couldn't do that with Bernie hanging on to her and whining. That's what it was. Why, she'll be back by nighttime tomorrow, or by the next day at the very latest.* Yeah, and what was that about "one week at the most"? *Okay, maybe a week. It takes a while to really move out of a place you've been in for nearly a year.*

Angel turned to the other side. It was no use. She wouldn't be able to sleep. Well, at least Bernie was still asleep. He didn't know Mama was gone. Oh Lord, what would happen when he found out? She wouldn't tell him. When he woke up tomorrow, she'd just say that Verna had to go to Burlington to clean out the apartment and that she'd be back soon. Meanwhile, she wanted them to be good and help their great-grandma.

Maybe they should just call the old lady Grandma. She was really Wayne's grandma, not hers and Bernie's, but Great-grandma took so long to say and sounded funny anyhow. Bernie seemed to like her—well, as much as Bernie liked any stranger. At least he wasn't scared of her. Angel had thought at first he might be. Good thing she'd remembered in time and hadn't told him the rest of the story of Hansel and Gretel. She wished she hadn't remembered it herself. This house wasn't made of gingerbread, that was for sure. Somehow she had to persuade Grandma to buy something besides canned peaches and pork and beans. She didn't seem to care a mosquito bite about proper nutrition, and since Bernie wasn't going to eat the beans, he'd only be eating one of the five major food groups. A little boy was likely to get sickly and die eating only canned peaches.

Shoot, Verna would be back long before that. She'd come with huge grocery bags full of good, nutritious things to eat. *You're nothing but a worrywart, Angel.* That's what Verna always said, and Angel did worry too much. She knew that. But she couldn't help it.

Maybe she should check Verna's bed. How could she be sure that was Verna's pickup she'd heard, anyway? It might belong to the guy she and Bernie had seen in the yard. Grandma must have known who he was. She wasn't worried a bit about someone prowling around. That was it. The truck she heard belonged to Grandma's Santy Claus. What was the matter with the old woman that she couldn't just say right out who it was? You had to admit she was a little weird—not scary weird, but old-lady weird.

Angel turned over in bed again. She really couldn't sleep. Maybe she should check Verna's bed and, if it was empty, go downstairs just to make sure Verna wasn't down there or outside smoking a cigarette or something. It was stupid to get all upset over nothing. And it *would* be nothing. Even if she had forgotten them in the diner that time, Verna wasn't going to run off and leave them like some silly teenage mother who didn't care. She loved Angel and Bernie, even if she did get mad at them sometimes.

You couldn't blame Verna for getting mad. She had a hard life. Wayne was in jail, so she had to earn enough money to take care of all three of them, and it wasn't easy getting a good job when you were a high school dropout with two kids and your husband was in jail. She was bound to get tired and worn down and lose her temper. Anybody would.

Angel slipped out from under the quilt and tiptoed around Bernie's bed. He had thrown his covers off and was sleeping on his back with his mouth open, making little squeaky noises. Angel pulled the quilt up and patted his shoulder. He grabbed the quilt and turned over with a big sigh.

At the door across the hall she peered in. The bedclothes were flat on the double bed. No Verna there. She patted around for the stair rail and felt her way carefully down the almost black staircase. The kitchen was dark and empty. Grandma had gotten out of her rocker and gone to bed. Maybe Verna had gone outside. Lots of times she went outdoors to smoke, especially when Angel reminded her of the dangers of secondhand smoke.

She crept over to the door. The floor creaked. She stopped, but there was no noise from behind the closed door to what must be Grandma's bedroom. She turned the knob of the kitchen door and pulled. See? It wasn't locked. If Grandma wasn't expecting Verna back soon, she would have locked the door, wouldn't she?

Verna was nowhere to be seen. There was no sign of the pickup, either. Angel walked farther out into the yard, just to make sure. And then for no reason at all she looked up and gasped.

She had never seen such a sight in her life. The sky was alive with stars. Some places were just great splotches of brilliant light. There wasn't just one star to wish on, there was a whole sky full. They blinked and gleamed as though they were inviting her to send a million wishes up to them.

First, I wish Verna would come home right now this minute. Or at least by morning. Second, I wish Bernie's evil wish would go away and Daddy would really come home and we'd all be happy and live in a real house in a real town. She moved away from the house, passed the hulking shape of a shed, and gingerly picked her way across the junk-filled yard, then through a gap in a broken-down fence and out into a field. She shivered in her thin pajamas, realizing too late that she should have put on her sneakers. The ground was rough and uneven, and it pricked and poked her feet, but she couldn't help it. It was like she was enchanted, like the sky had put a spell on her. She forgot about Verna, about Wayne, even about Bernie, and just stood there with her head bent back to her spine, staring.

"Beautiful, isn't it?"

Angel jumped. The man was right behind her, towering over her. He was taller than Wayne. She turned around. She couldn't see his face clearly, but it was framed by a shaggy beard and unkempt hair. *Santy Claus.* A little flip of fear twanged against her stomach.

"Don't you love it?"

She couldn't say anything at all. His head was back now, looking at the sky. He had the huge thing she had thought of as a bazooka in his big left hand. "Come with me," he said, straightening up. "Let me show you something."

Angel knew better than to follow strangers. Good Lord, they lectured about it at school all the time. She shook her head. "No. No, I have to go in," she added, in case he couldn't see her shaking her head in the dark. "Right now." She turned to go, careful not to touch him as she passed.

"I was just going to take a close look at Jupiter," he said. "I bet you never saw Jupiter through a telescope."

So that was what the bazooka was: a telescope. She *was* tempted, but no kid with any sense would let someone she didn't know— "I gotta go in," she said again, but she was no longer moving in that direction.

"You don't remember me, do you, Angel?" How did he know her name? "When you were just a tiny thing, I held you up so you could look at the stars through my telescope. That was my old telescope. I've got a better one now."

Something stirred inside Angel. Was that the good

thing that had happened to her here? There had been a fight, and she had run out—out of the trailer and into the field. Someone had been there who picked her up and took her to see the stars. She remembered it as a dream with an angel sent from God when she was small and frightened.

"Yes, I do. I remember," she said.

She followed the tall man out into the middle of the pasture. There were no trees, no buildings, no animals or people there—only the earth and the sky. He put the telescope down on its long skinny legs and twisted little screws until he had it standing firm. Then he put his eye to a little short tube on top and moved the long tube slowly until he said, "Okay, here she is. In all her splendor, Angel. I think she wants to show off for you tonight." He stepped back. "Now, put your eye right here." He indicated the end of the long tube. "That's it. Do you see it?"

She didn't see anything but black. "No," she said. "I'm sorry."

He bent his own eye to the tube and twisted a knob on the side. "Now try," he said.

"Oh," she breathed, "ooh. It's got four babies!"

He laughed. "Those 'babies' are really moons. Poor old earth only has one, but Jupiter has a whole string of them and a lot of dust as well. My 'scope isn't powerful enough to show more than those four." He put his hand on her shoulder. "You see that great big splotch of light over there?"

She hated to take her eye away from the telescope to look, but she did because he asked her to. "Yeah?"

"What do you think that is?"

"I don't know," she said. "A really huge star?"

"That's what it looks like, but it's a cluster of stars. Not just one. And do you know how far away they are from you right now?"

"A thousand miles?"

"No. More like millions of miles. We're not even looking at stars. We're looking at the light from stars so far away it takes the light from the nearest star about two million years to travel from that star to your eye. And that light is going at 186,000 miles a second."

She felt dizzy when she put her eye to the eyepiece again. How could she believe what he was saying? It wasn't stars she was seeing at all—just the light of stars zooming like fury to get to the earth but taking forever because it was so far to go.

She stepped back, moving her eye from the eyepiece and the overwhelming thought of light streaming down from fiery worlds whirling in space beyond all human view. "It's scary," she said.

"What's scary?"

"How big everything is—how far away. I'd just be like an ant to that star."

"Nah. Not nearly that big," he said. "The whole world isn't that big."

"You mean we're like nothing? The whole world is

like nothing?" It frightened her to think of herself—her whole world—like less than a speck in the gigantic sky, like nothing at all.

"Yeah, we're small, but we aren't nothing," he said. "Want to know a secret?"

"What?"

He reached over and pinched her arm.

"Ow," she said. It didn't hurt so much as surprise her.

"See this?" he said, lifting her arm up where he'd pinched it. "See this stuff here? This is the stuff of stars."

"What do you mean?"

"The same elements, the same materials that make those stars up there is what makes you. You're made from star stuff."

It didn't make sense. "They're burning in the sky, and I'm just standing here, not shining at all."

"Well, yes, but that doesn't mean you're made from different stuff. Just that something different is happening to those same elements. You're still close kin to the stars."

She was trembling out there in the August night in nothing but her pajamas, but it wasn't because of the cold. "I better go in," she said. "Bernie might wake up and miss me." She started picking her way back toward the house, turning only when she got to the cluttered safety of the yard. She could see the tall shadowed form standing there, watching her, like a person from a strange dream.

EIGHT

Treasure Hunt

When she woke, the sun was streaming through the small window. For a minute Angel couldn't remember where she was. Stars. There was something about stars, a dream of stars and a strange man who knew them all by name. A little thrill went through her body, and then she looked down at the patchwork cover, and the crazy quilt of a day that had brought her to this house and to this bed came rushing to mind. She sat up and craned her neck, trying to see into the room across the hall, but she couldn't see well enough to tell for sure whether someone was in the bed or not.

She made her way around Bernie, gently snoring in his bed, and crossed to the room that was meant to be Verna's. The door hung slightly open. Was that the way Angel had left it last night? She was sure she had shut it, which would mean . . . She pushed it gently with her fingertips. It creaked. She held her breath. There was no one in the bed. It had not been slept in. She lifted the quilt. Verna hadn't even put sheets on the bed. No use trying to fool herself. Verna had not returned last night.

She went back into her bedroom—she would have to

get used to thinking of it as hers, hers and Bernie's—and pulled on her clothes, all the while keeping an eye on Bernie's curled-up hump. Grizzle had fallen onto the floor and was staring up at her with his big button eyes, as though asking what in the world had happened that he should suffer so. She picked him up, dusted him with her hand, and then tucked him under the cover beside Bernie. The boy shifted slightly, as though making room.

From down in the kitchen came the sound of heavy footsteps. Grandma was up and about. Good. She hated to think that the old woman spent her entire life in that rocker. With her sneakers in her hand, she crept down the stairs. At the bottom she paused long enough to shove her sockless feet into the loosely tied sneakers. She wiped her hands on the back of her jeans.

Grandma turned from the stove as Angel came into the room. "You're up, eh?"

She nodded.

"Well, make yourself useful."

She wanted to, she really did, but she had no idea what the old woman would want her to do. She was scared to ask questions like "Where is the cereal?" There probably wasn't any.

"You know where the spoons are, don't you?"

"Yes," she answered and hurried over to get three out and put them on the table.

"Looks like Santy Claus brung you some breakfast things," Grandma said, waving at a brown bag sitting on the counter. "See what you can find in there." She plopped herself into the rocker. "I'm wore out already and I ain't even made my coffee."

"I can make coffee." Angel said it before she realized that making coffee at Grandma's might be different from making it in the apartment.

"It's just the powder kind," Grandma said, waving at the hot plate. "The water's probably hot enough."

There was a jar of instant coffee open on the counter, and beside it a stained saucerless cup. Angel got another spoon and carefully put a heaping spoonful into the cup. An old wooden-handled kettle was noisily gurgling on the hot plate. She took it off and carefully poured the water into the cup. She could tell at once that the water hadn't really boiled; the coffee was a funny cloudy color. Verna would have poured it down the sink. "Do you want milk or sugar?" she asked timidly.

"Three spoons of sugar and a splash of milk, if there's some in that bag over there."

Angel found the sugar pretty quickly. It was near the stove in a big canister with a handmade label that said SUGAR. She looked into the grocery bag, and sure enough, there was a half gallon of 2 percent milk and a box of sug-ared cereal—not Sugar Pops, but maybe Bernie wouldn't mind too much. At least it would be a change from beans and canned peaches.

Angel handed Grandma the cup, trying to figure out how to ask about Verna. She could have asked right out, but anxious as to what the answer might be, she put off asking, busying herself by putting the milk into the fridge.

"That brother of yours always sleep this late?"

"I guess he was pretty tired."

"I heard you scurrying around like a little mouse last night. What was you up to?"

"I heard the pickup. It woke me up."

"So you went chasing after that woman, eh?"

How was Angel to answer that? "I guess she left some things behind that she had to go get."

Grandma made a funny sound with her lips that sounded like "Pagh!"

"Bernie'll be worried when he wakes up and she's not here."

"I know just how Bernie might feel. I was somewhat agitated myself," she said, rocking so hard Angel feared the coffee would come sloshing out of the cup onto her lap.

"Didn't she tell you she was leaving?" Angel couldn't keep the worry out of her voice.

"Not in so many words. I guess I shoulda known, but I ain't as sharp"—Grandma tapped her temple—"as I once was. That Verna pulled a fast one, all right."

"I'm sure she'll be back soon," Angel said, her stomach plunging.

"Yeah?" Grandma leaned forward, bracing her feet on the floor. "Then what was all that about how she had to get on with the rest of her life? I think that worthless girl just deserted her husband in jail *and* dumped her two kids on an old woman hardly got the strength to take care of herself anymore. Oh Lordy, like they say, history repeats itself. Just like that useless daughter-in-law of mine, running off and leaving me with Wayne, and him hardly more than a baby."

"Verna wouldn't leave us! I swear she wouldn't. She loves Bernie and me!"

"Not near as much as she loves Verna Morgan."

"What you yelling about?" Bernie was standing in the doorway, one arm clutching the blue bear, the other fist rubbing his nose.

"You're up, Bernie."

"Where's Mama?" He was looking around the kitchen. When his gaze got to Grandma, she humphed and looked down at her cup. He turned back to Angel. "I said, Where's Mama?"

"She just had to run back to the apartment and clean it out and stuff," Angel said, daring Grandma to contradict her. "She'll be back as soon as she can." To her relief, he seemed content with her answer, at least for now. "Want some cereal? It's not Sugar Pops, but it's just as good."

He sat down where she indicated he should and let the bear slide to the floor beside him. Angel picked it up, started to dust it off, and, thinking better of that, arranged the bear in the chair next to Bernie. She opened the box and shook out a bowlful of cereal, poured milk on it, and handed him the bowl and a spoon. "Here."

"I need sugar."

"It's already got sugar, Bernie. It's coated with sugar. You don't need any more. It's bad for your teeth."

"I *do* need some more." She couldn't afford to have him upset, so she put on a scant teaspoonful from the sugar jar.

"Spoiled as last year's apples, that boy," the old woman muttered. Angel ignored her.

If Bernie was spoiled, it was probably all her fault. She wanted him to be happy, that was all. He got unhappy so quickly. She poured herself a bowl of the pink sugared balls, remembering to put the milk away in the fridge before sitting down across from Bernie. He wasn't eating.

"Yuck," he said. "It tastes terrible."

"Do you want *beans,* then?" She kept her tone low but fierce.

He shook his head and bent over the bowl.

Whatever was she going to do with him? With herself, for that matter? It wasn't fair. What could Verna be thinking of, leaving her and Bernie here? She forced herself to chew the too-sweet soggy blobs. The cereal smelled like perfume. She wanted to stop eating it, but whenever she started to put down the spoon, she could feel Bernie watching her. Finally, she whispered across the table to him, "It's all there is right now, Bernie. I know Mama will bring you some Sugar Pops when she comes back."

He squinched his face into a hard little knot.

"Try to be good," she pleaded softly. "Ple-e-eeze."

He didn't say anything, but to her relief, he took another bite of the terrible cereal.

When they finished, or almost finished, they'd both left a half-dozen sodden lumps swimming in the now pink milk at the bottom of the bowl. Angel stood up and said loudly, "I'll just rinse these out, all right, Bernie? Then you and me can go outside and play for a while."

He looked at her in a puzzled way but didn't speak. Instead, he reached over and dragged the bear to himself. The right thumb went into his mouth. She gave her head a little shake, but he was not to be denied this comfort.

"How old are you, boy?" Grandma's sharp voice exclaimed. "I never saw such a big boy with his thumb jammed down his throat."

Angel moved more quickly to the sink. She poured the rest of the pink milk into it without bothering to strain out the lumps. Quickly rinsing the bowls, she put them face-down on the counter beside the sink. "Okay, Bernie. Ready to go out?"

"I'm still in my jammies."

She started to say that in the country it didn't matter if he was in his birthday suit, but she thought better of it. "Okay. Upstairs, then."

He was no help as she tried to get his pajamas off and urge him into his clothes. He insisted on holding on to the bear, and she had to yank it from his grasp before she could get his pajama sleeve off. Putting on his T-shirt was impossible.

"Want a new T-shirt?" she asked.

"No."

"Okay. I was going to give you my genuine Disney World Goofy T-shirt, but since you don't . . ."

"Okay. Okay. Okay. I'll take it."

She got the shirt out of her suitcase. "You don't get it unless you put Grizzle down long enough for me to put it on you."

"Okay," he said, as though angry that he had to do this huge favor for her. He threw the bear on the floor.

"You keep dropping Grizzle on the floor and he might just run away from home." It was out of her mouth before she thought. She could see his face cloud up, and then he began to cry. Not loud, like a tantrum, but little sucking, sobbing sounds as though his heart would break.

"I told you, Bernie," Angel said, kneeling beside him, putting her arms around him and pulling him close. "I told you, she's just gone for a little while. She'll be back soon."

"No, she won't," he blubbered into the T-shirt. "She's run away and she's never coming back. Never. Never. Never." He gulped and wiped his nose on the back of his hand. "And it's all my fault, 'cause I was bad."

"She *is* coming back, Bernie. I promise. And you weren't bad."

"I was. I was. I was. I wanted a milk shake. She promised me a milk shake. That's why I was so bad. She *prom-ised*."

"I know, Bernie. I know. But people can't always keep their promises. Even when they want to." She remembered too late that *she* had just promised that Mama would come home soon. "But Mama *will* come home soon. That's a really true promise. I promise you."

He looked up at her suspiciously. "How do you know it's true?"

"I just know it, okay? Here." She looked around for a tissue box and, seeing none, dug into her jeans pocket and found a tissue mostly in shreds. She wiped his runny nose with it the best she could. He didn't resist as she finished dressing him.

★　★　★　★　★

"Now what?" asked Bernie as they stood outside in the bright sunshine of the yard, looking over at piles of junk and the old broken-down shed. It was a good question.

"Bernie, we are on a make-your-own adventure."

"What's that?"

"Well, I read about it in this book at school. You find yourself someplace weird and you, well, you just look around and decide what to do next. Then what you decide leads you into a big adventure."

"I don't want to play that," he said, sticking his thumb back into his mouth.

"Okay. Then I'll just go off and play by myself." Angel started toward the pasture. In the daylight she could see that it lay beyond what had been once a rail fence. Most of the rails lay rotting on the ground. In daytime there would be nothing to see in the pasture, no stars, no planets, but it was safer to walk around in than this junk-filled yard.

"Wait!" he said. She turned.

Bernie was running toward her in a zigzag pattern around the junk, dragging poor Grizzle in the dirt behind him.

"Why don't we leave Grizzle here while we go on our adventure?"

"No!" he said. "Grizzle would hate that. He'd be scared."

"Okay, but don't drag him around, okay? He's getting filthy."

Bernie looked down at the bear. "He's too heavy to carry."

"Well, let me carry him, then."

Reluctantly, he handed over the bear. "You won't ever leave him, will you?"

"No, I promise." That word again. Luckily, he let it pass.

The pasture was much smaller than it had seemed to her last night. There were no cows or sheep in it, as there had been in the pastures they passed yesterday. The grass was stubby, and the occasional prickle bush dotted the hilly ground. There was no sign that the farm on Morgan Farm Road existed anymore. There wasn't even a barn.

Just the old house, the junk-filled yard, the broken-down trailer, and the small, empty field, which was beautiful at night but poor and scrabbly in daylight. On the far side of the field there was a wood, but she didn't feel adventurous enough to lead Bernie and Grizzle into the woods. What if they got lost? They'd never be able to find their way back.

"I don't like it here," Bernie said, reaching for Grizzle. "There's nothing to do and nothing to eat and nobody to play with. Nothing. Nothing. Nothing." He rubbed his cheek against the blue plush.

"Sure there is, Bernie. I choose the adventure of going into the yard and trying to discover hidden treasure."

"What hidden treasure?"

"In those piles of junk in the yard there lies a wonderful treasure, just waiting for you and me to discover it."

"You're lying!"

"Okay. Go on back into the house. I'll go on this adventure all by myself."

"I don't want to go in the house."

"Suit yourself." Angel headed back to the yard. He followed her, trailing Grizzle along behind him. She pretended not to see.

The chief junk pile was a small hill of rusting metal. She guessed it was discarded farm machinery of some sort. She was afraid to touch it. You got terrible diseases if you cut yourself on rusty metal, didn't you? Lockjaw or something. "This is the wrong pile for treasure," she said as Bernie caught up with her.

"How do you know?"

"I just know," she said. "I choose we explore the shed."

"How come you get to choose?"

"Because I'm the biggest."

"You're always the biggest."

She ignored him and picked her way around the yard to the small shed. The door sagged like it was worn out from trying to stand up straight for too many years. There was an encrusted orangy latch that could no longer fasten, from which drooped a useless lock, its rusted shackle hanging open. She pulled at the door, but the bottom was embedded in dirt and it didn't move. She gave it a tremendous jerk, yanking it wide enough open to peer in. "It's like the door to the Secret Garden," she whispered.

"What garden?"

She didn't answer.

NINE

A Is for Astronomy

The shed, as Angel might have guessed, was piled with junk, but there was enough space for the two children to slip in. There was a small dirty window on either side and, to her surprise, light coming in from above. Not from an unpatched hole, but from a little tower with holes as though someone had put them there on purpose. Then she remembered the fourth-grade field trip to see maple syrup being made. That building had a tower with holes in it to let steam and smoke rising from the boiling sap escape. So what she'd thought was a shed in Grandma's yard was really a sugar shack, long past its maple sugaring days. Around the walls the children could see stacks of old papers and magazines, a baby bed, a highchair, something that might once have been a lawn mower, rusting sap buckets and large metal pans. In the middle, loaded down with more papers, was the old boiling stove, a piece of rusted pipe still hanging from the wall.

Bernie wrinkled up his nose. "It stinks in here."

It did smell in the shed, like mold and rot, and something sickly sweet, left over from its days of glory when sap had boiled down to syrup on the stove.

"I don't like it in here," Bernie said. He began to wheeze. At the clinic they had told Verna to watch for signs of asthma.

"Go back outside," Angel commanded. She meant to follow him, but something caught her eye: a line of books, tall volumes that had once been maroon, now multicolored with mold. She pushed aside a stack of buckets to get close enough to see what they were.

"An-gel," Bernie whined from the open door.

"Just a minute. Just a minute." They were old encyclopedias. But the sky wouldn't have changed, would it? She searched the shelves for the S volume—something that would tell her about the stars. The volumes were all out of order, so she ran the point of her fingernail across the numbers and letters until she found *Sordello – Textbooks* and began frantically to flip through the musty pages, trying to ignore Bernie, whose whining was getting louder.

Between "Star Chamber," which was not about stars at all and "Starfish," which might look like a star but wasn't one any more than she was, there was a long article about "Star Clusters." She could tell it was way beyond what she could understand. Bernie was blamming on the side of the shed, but she couldn't stop now. "Okay. Okay. I just need a minute."

"That's what you always say!"

She didn't bother to argue. Her eyes raced down the page. At the end of the article it said: *See* Nebula;

Astrophysics; Astronomy. Of course, astronomy. That was what she wanted.

"An-*gel!*"

"Hold your pants on, Bernie. I said I wouldn't be a minute."

"You already been lots of minutes."

"Well, you just got to wait a few more minutes." Why was it you could always find everything except the one thing you had to have? There was Volume 1, but it stopped with "Antarctic."

"I'm warning you, Angel Morgan, you better get out here this minute. Or . . . or else!"

There it was! She pulled out the heavy volume and turned quickly, setting the pile of buckets clattering about. She picked her way around them—no time to stack them upright again—and came out of the shed panting, as though she had just finished a long race.

Bernie eyed her and the big book with suspicion. "I'm telling," he said.

"What?"

"I'm telling Grandma you're stealing her book."

"I'm not stealing. I'm just borrowing it. Like from a library."

"You are, too, stealing and you know it."

"Oh, Bernie. I'm just moving it from the shed to the house. It's not even leaving the property. Don't tell, okay, Bernie?"

"If you're not stealing, how come I can't tell?"

It took her a minute to come up with an answer. "Grandma doesn't know us very well yet, see? She might not understand. She might not want us going into the shed at all."

"I'm not going in anymore. I don't like it, and it makes me breathe funny."

"You don't have to go inside anymore, but you might want me to."

"Why?"

She paused and looked at him, Grizzle dangling from his left hand, his right hand on his hip, challenging her. "Because there might be a hidden treasure in there or something."

"A treasure?" The hand popped off his hip. "A real one? Not just pretend?"

"Uh-huh."

"If there was, would you share?"

"Of course I would. Don't I always share with you, Bernie? Still," she added, "we'd have to tell Grandma."

"Why?" His eyes went wide.

"Because," she said, "if we didn't, it would be like stealing."

"No, it wouldn't! If we find it, it's our treasure. That's the law."

"But you just said if I took the book—"

"Books are different."

"Well, just to be on the safe side, maybe we better not say anything about the book, either, okay?"

"Okay," he said, jamming his thumb into his mouth.

★   ★   ★   ★   ★

They waited until they were sure that Grandma was not in the kitchen before they sneaked in. They carried the book upstairs. Angel slid it under her pillow. She took a look around the room. "We better make up our beds, Bernie."

"Why? Grandma won't care. She never comes up here. She said so."

"Because it looks nicer to have your bed neat."

"Then you do it," he said, turning on his heel and marching downstairs, still dragging the bear. He was going to ruin Grizzle, she knew, but how could she save the bear and still keep Bernie from throwing a fit? She sighed and began to make the beds. The bottom sheet wasn't fitted, so it was hard to do the corners and smooth the covers, but with the quilts on top, the wrinkles didn't show so much.

She could hear Bernie downstairs talking to Grandma, so she slipped the encyclopedia out from under her pillow and looked for "Astronomy." The print was small, and there were no real pictures, just scientific drawings, but she'd have to try. "Astronomy is the most ancient of sciences, having existed before the dawn of recorded civilizations." She let out a long sigh as though she'd been holding her breath all her life. She was about to embark on a mysterious make-your-own adventure. She was

about to go back "before the dawn of recorded civilizations."

★ ★ ★ ★ ★

"Angel. Angel. An-*gel!*" Bernie was leaning over her.
"Wake up!"

She sat up on the bed. She must have fallen asleep
over the heavy book. "I'm awake," she said. "I was reading."

"No, you wasn't. You was snoring."

"What do you want, Bernie? I'm really busy right now."

"Grandma says if we want something to eat besides
beans and peaches and that yucky cereal, you got to walk
to the store."

"Okay." She sat up quickly, shoving the book once
more under her pillow.

"She says *you* got to go. She thinks I'm too *little* to go
by myself." His bottom lip stuck out a mile.

"We got to go together," she said. "I need you to help
carry things." She stood up and pulled down her T-shirt.
"Is she going to give us some money?" she asked.

He shrugged. "I guess so."

Grandma handed Angel a five-dollar bill. Not enough,
Angel knew, for much in the way of groceries. But it
would get them through the day. Verna would surely be
back tonight—or tomorrow at the latest. Surely.

It was about two miles to the store, Grandma had
said, well beyond the old house where Verna had stopped
for directions, all the way back to the village they had

come past. Still, it was a beautiful late-summer day, not too hot, and what else could she do to entertain Bernie? She made him leave Grizzle behind. "You can't carry groceries *and* a bear at the same time," she told him.

They started up the road in good spirits, but long before they got to the house where Verna had asked for directions, Bernie began dragging his feet and complaining. "I'm too hot and tired," he said. "Why doesn't Grandma drive us to the store?"

"She doesn't have a car," Angel said. "She's probably too old to drive anyway."

"She does, too, have a car, " he said. "Over by the trailer."

"I didn't see any car."

"Well, I did. I saw it yesterday when we got here. A big old dirty car over on the other side of that trailer."

"It's probably just junk—like the trailer. In the country, if a car breaks down, people just leave it to rust away. They don't bother taking it to a junkyard."

"Why wasn't it there this morning, then?"

Angel stopped still in the road. "Bernie, you saw a car there yesterday, and this morning it was gone?"

"I just said I did, didn't I?"

Maybe the star man wasn't a dream. "Maybe—"

"What?"

"Nothing, Bernie. I guess somebody lives in the trailer, that's all." She started walking again, but Bernie didn't move.

"Angel!" She turned. The pout on his face had been replaced by fear. "Suppose it's the robber? The one with the big gun?"

"That wasn't a robber. You heard Grandma."

"She said it was Santa Claus. That was a lie, for sure."

"Well, whoever it was, it's nobody that's going to hurt us."

"How do you know? He had that big gun."

She went back and took his hand. "It probably wasn't a gun, Bernie."

He snatched away his hand. "Then what was it if it wasn't a gun? Just tell me that!"

Why couldn't she say "telescope"? Why couldn't she just tell him about the star man? Instead, she said, "Well, what if it *was* a gun? Lots of people in the country have guns. That doesn't mean they're crazy or that they want to shoot you. People in the country like to hunt and stuff." She took his hand again. "Tell you what. If they have Sugar Pops in the store, I promise I'll buy a box, okay?"

"You'll just say they're too 'spensive."

And she wanted to. In the country store, which smelled just a little less musty than the shed, Sugar Pops cost more than three dollars, and she had only five. But the chubby clerk had already climbed the ladder and gotten them down from a high shelf before she told Angel the price. Angel got a small jar of peanut butter and a loaf of bread with the rest of the money. That should get them through until Mama got back. There was no money for jelly, but it couldn't be helped. She had to buy the Sugar Pops for Bernie.

He was not particularly grateful. The store had rows of candy bars and a whole case full of Popsicles. "I need a Popsicle," Bernie said.

"We don't have enough money," Angel said as quietly as she could.

"Okay, then, how 'bout a candy bar."

"I can't, Bernie." If only she'd put the taxi money in her socks. It hadn't occurred to her that she would need emergency money out here in the country where there wasn't a taxi for miles around.

The clerk looked at her as though she felt sorry for her—no more money and a little brother who couldn't understand. Maybe she'd feel sorry enough to throw in a candy bar or something, but "Have a nice day, kids" was all she said when she smiled and handed Angel the few pennies of change, pushing the small bag of groceries across the counter at her.

Angel grabbed Bernie's hand and dragged him out of the store and down the steps. At the bottom, she put the bag on the ground and took out the Sugar Pops. She opened the box and handed Bernie a handful. "Here," she said. "It's just like candy."

"No, it's not," said Bernie, but he began eating it anyway, sucking each bit until it dissolved in his mouth. It kept him quiet for almost five minutes. *Oh Lord, what am I going to do if Mama doesn't come back tonight?*

★   ★   ★   ★   ★

Mama didn't come back that night—or the next night.

"You promised!" Bernie accused her. "You said she'd be right back."

"I know, Bernie. I don't know what's keeping her."

"She's never coming back. Never. Never. Never."

She tried calling their old number. Grandma's phone was an old black one attached to the kitchen wall. It was a dial phone with numbers in a circle instead of buttons to push. She knew it was long distance, and she felt bad about using Grandma's phone for long distance, but she couldn't help it. She had to try. The phone just rang and rang. The third day someone answered. It wasn't Verna. It was the machine operator voice saying, "This is no longer a working number." That meant Verna had settled every-thing, moved out, and was on the way back! "See, Bernie, I told you. She'll be here tonight."

★   ★   ★   ★   ★

But she wasn't back that night, or the next. Still, she'd promised Grandma— "No more than a week." The week passed. No Verna. They'd run out of Sugar Pops, since Bernie ate them for every meal, not just breakfast. Angel made herself eat the other sugared stuff at breakfast and ate peanut butter sandwiches for the rest of the meals. Grandma was content with beans and canned peaches. It didn't seem the time or the place for Angel to explain about the five major food groups and how even older adults needed to have a balanced diet.

She made the milk last almost the whole week, rationing it out on breakfast cereal and never drinking it otherwise. Bernie didn't care about milk anyhow. He was content to eat his Sugar Pops dry at lunch and supper. He regularly asked for soda, but it was more to annoy her than a real request. Angel knew he didn't really think a Pepsi was going to magically appear in the fridge. But those dry, sticky peanut butter sandwiches made Angel long for a tall glass of cool milk herself. She'd never thought of how much she liked milk before. She dreamed about milk. It was almost like people lost in the desert imagining they see an oasis.

To top it all, it rained every day that week. What was she going to do? Bernie was nagging at her every minute. If only there was a TV. Who cared what Ms. Hallingford thought about TV rotting little minds? Angel was about to lose her own mind with nothing around to keep Bernie quiet. Secretly, she searched the house, including the closed-up sitting room, every room but Grandma's bedroom, but she couldn't find a set. She made no progress in her venture into astronomy. Bernie claimed whenever she pulled the book out that it made him wheeze.

Finally, on Saturday morning, when there was still no Verna, she went to the phone before anyone else was awake. She put her index finger in the 1 and dragged it heavily around until it stopped. Then she let go, and when the 1 was back in place, started on the 8, laboriously pulling her finger around all ten numbers, calling

the only phone number besides her own that she had
ever memorized, the one she'd carried around, like the
taxi money in her pocket, for emergency use only.

"I need to speak to Mr. Wayne Morgan," she said to
the operator who answered. "This is his daughter. It's an
emergency."

The Swan

The operator wouldn't call Wayne to the phone. She took Angel's number and said she would give him the message to call. But the phone didn't ring. Come to think of it, she hadn't heard the phone ring the whole time she and Bernie had been at Grandma's. Maybe it didn't work. Maybe Wayne was trying and trying to call back, but the phone was broken and he couldn't get through.

When a whole day and evening had passed and still no call, Angel finally blurted out her worry to Grandma. She waited the next morning until Bernie had gone into the bathroom. She shut the door firmly behind him, held tightly on to the knob behind her back, and said quietly, "Grandma, I think your phone's broke."

"Nothing wrong with that phone. Just old. Not one of your fancy-dancy kinds, but it works fine. What's the matter? You trying to make phone calls without asking?"

She had been. Long distance, too. "I shoulda asked. But I had to call Daddy."

"Wayne? You tried to call Wayne at the jail?"

"Yes, I did. I should have asked you, but I was so worried about Mama not coming back—"

"So that's why he called last night."

"He called?" Her voice went up to a squeak. "Why didn't you tell me?"

"You was asleep. Besides, the dang fool tried to call collect. I ain't accepting charges for no long-distance phone call. The woman said would I accept a collect call from Wayne Morgan, and I said, 'Not on your stuffed cabbage. If that boy wants to call he can do it on his own nickel, not his poor old grandma's.'"

"Grandma! I need to talk to Daddy!"

"What about?"

"Mama. I got to talk to him about Mama. She's gone, and I don't know where she's at or when she's coming back. I need to ask him what me and Bernie are supposed to do."

"Do?" the old woman cocked her head. "What do you mean, *do?*"

"We can't stay here, Grandma. It isn't fair to you, and—and— Well, what if Welfare finds us and puts us in foster care? What will happen to us then?" She fought back the tears that were threatening to choke her.

"You silly girl. Ain't no Welfare woman gonna get you."

"But Grandma, if they came here . . ." How was she supposed to explain that this was no fit home for children? "Grandma, children need— Well, growing children need the five major food groups, for one thing."

"The five major *what?*"

"Let me outta here!" Bernie was kicking the bathroom door. She moved away, and he fell into the kitchen. "You trying to keep me in jail?" he asked her accusingly.

"No," she said, and then the tears came. "I'm trying to keep you outta jail, Bernie Morgan. I don't want you to grow up to be a criminal and leave your wife and b-b-b-break your children's hearts."

Bernie looked at her in astonishment. "You not supposed to cry, Angel."

"Well, I *am* crying, so there."

"Oh, hush, hush, the both of you," said Grandma. "Anybody got a right to cry around here, it's me. And you don't see me blubbering, now do you?"

"Grandmas don't cry," said Bernie. "Just little kids. So stop crying this minute, Angel. You're too big to cry."

She wanted to stop, but she couldn't. Finally, she turned and ran upstairs and threw herself down on the bed and just boo-hooed big shuddering, slobbery sobs into the thin pillow until it was soaked. In one part of her mind she was watching herself and knew she was getting a strange pleasure out of this uncontrolled wailing—as though a huge plug had been pulled and an ocean of the fears and worries and all the unspent tears of her life were pouring out of her in one torrential flood.

Too soon Bernie was standing over her, making worried little noises.

"Angel. Angel. *An-gel!* Stop it, you hear?"

But she didn't stop. Couldn't stop. Didn't even want

to stop. It felt too good to let loose, not to be in charge anymore—not of anything or anyone, including herself. She just might spend the rest of her days like this— crying her miserable life away—with nobody expecting her to be responsible for anything ever again.

"Bernie?" Dimly she could hear Grandma's voice from the bottom of the stairs. "You leave her alone, all right? Come on down and I'll fix us some breakfast."

She could hear Bernie shuffling his feet, trying to decide whether or not to obey. But she wasn't going to tell him what to do. She was not in charge anymore.

"I'm going down now, Angel, you hear? And as soon as you stop acting like a baby, you come down, too, okay? You hear me?"

She didn't even bother to nod. He hesitated a minute and then started out of the room. "Crying ain't going to get you nothing, you know."

She would have laughed except crying felt too good to interrupt. Then she heard him walk over to his own bed and felt him lift her arm and shove Grizzle under it. She grabbed the bear tightly, buried her face in his soft blue stomach, and just lay curled up there like a baby, hollering her insides out. "When you can control your-self, you can come down and have some breakfast with Grandma and me, okay?" he said before clomping down the stairs.

At last it was over. Her body was as limp as laundry after the spin cycle. From downstairs she could hear the drone of Grandma's voice and the high staccato of Bernie's. She hugged Grizzle close, stuck her thumb in her mouth, and fell sound asleep.

★   ★   ★   ★   ★

She woke up, her eyes puffy, her mouth dry and cottony. She didn't know what time it was or even where she was. She sat up slowly. Grizzle was on the floor next to the bed. She picked him up and automatically dusted him off. She was going to have to take a dust mop to this floor, that was for sure. No wonder Bernie's allergies were acting up.

She stood up, still not really sure what had happened to her. Something important, she knew that much. She felt heavy from the unnatural daytime sleep. She couldn't remember ever going to bed in the daytime. And hungry. Her stomach felt plastered against her backbone. Somehow the thought of going downstairs filled her with dread. Why? Then she remembered. She'd made a fool of herself. She'd bawled and screeched and howled like a maniac—and it had felt wonderful. She ought to be ashamed. The real Angel Morgan would be mortified. But she wasn't. Instead, she was, as Verna would say, "going to put it all behind me and get on with the rest of my life," whatever that might mean.

The two of them looked up from the table when she appeared at the door, both like little puppies waiting to see if they were going to be kicked or petted.

"Are you eating those dang Sugar Pops again, Bernie?

I swear, you're going to keel right over from sugar over-
dose."

"So?" he said, his chin belligerent, his eyes full of
relief.

"*So* we gotta get some meat and vegetables into you,
don't we, Grandma?"

"I get my Social Security check this week," the old
woman said meekly. "Can you wait till then for the shopping?"

"I guess I'll have to," Angel said primly. They wanted
her to be in charge, both of them. That was who she was
doomed to be, the responsible one. Deep down that was
who she wanted to be, wasn't it? Not that baby up there
on the bed, crying and sucking her thumb.

She sighed silently. The rest of her life was going to be
just like all the days since that thrilling one when the new-
born Bernie had been put into her arms. "Take care of your
baby brother now, Angel," Verna had said. Angel hadn't
known then what that meant. Now she did. The thrill was
long gone, but the duty had become like the sun in the
solar system, the center around which all the other parts of
her life revolved. Without it, she would likely fly to pieces.

She looked at the two faces turned toward her, waiting for her to tell them that everything was going to be all
right. Now she had two troubled, troublesome children
to look out for. She straightened up. "I guess I'll get me
some breakfast now," she said.

"Hmmph," said Grandma. "Better call it lunch."

★   ★   ★   ★   ★

Sometime while she had slept, the rain that had been coming down all week stopped. The sky was an almost magazine-picture blue. The first thing she was going to do was hang the wet laundry outside. Grandma had an old washing machine in her bathroom but no dryer, and yesterday she'd had to hang her and Bernie's wet clothes all over the house. She got the big woven basket from the bathroom and gathered underwear and T-shirts from around the edge of the bathtub and off the backs of kitchen chairs.

"C'mon, Bernie," she said, "we're going outside."

"I don't want to go outside," Bernie said. "There's nothing to do outside."

"I got to hang up the laundry. Besides, growing children need fresh air."

"Maybe I don't want to be a growing children," he said.

"Too bad. We're going out anyway." She propped the basket under one arm, grabbed his hand, and dragged him out the door.

"Want to help me hang these clothes up?"

"No."

She took clothespins out of the bag at the end of the clothesline and began to pin up the damp washing.

"That car is gone again," Bernie said.

She glanced over at the trailer. Could it be that the mysterious star man lived over there? That it was his car that appeared and disappeared as though he went to work every day like a regular person? She put the last pin on a pair of Bernie's underpants. Then, without a word, she started across the yard toward the broken-down trailer. Looking at it from Grandma's house, it didn't seem as if anyone could live in such a place, but if the star man was real and not just a dream, there was a chance that he might live in the trailer, wasn't there?

She felt daring crossing the weedy field, climbing over the broken-down fence, sneaking to the trailer. It was propped up on cinder blocks and looked unsteady, as if a slight breeze might just blow it off. There were rickety wooden steps leading to the door.

"Where you going, Angel?" Bernie was running to catch up with her.

"Shh. I just want to look—see if anybody lives in here."

"You better not! It might be the man with the gun. He'll shoot you dead if he catches you peeping in his house."

She ignored him, although her stomach gave a little flip at the thought of someone catching her in the act. Everyone knew it was against the law to be a Peeping Tom.

The little window set in the door was dirty. She wiped it hurriedly with her sleeve and put her face against the glass. The inside of the trailer was dark, and in the shadows she could see a dark couch, a tiny oil stove, a sink, and books. Lots of books. No one was in sight, but it must be the star man's house. Who else would have lots of books? Yes, there by the far wall was the long telescope, on its three legs. Barely breathing, she backed down the stairs. Bernie was standing several feet away, ready to run.

"You can relax, Bernie. Nobody's home."

"I wasn't scared," he said.

"I know you weren't. I was just saying that." And adding more to herself than to Bernie, "It wasn't a dream."

"What's not a dream?"

"Nothing." She didn't want to tell Bernie about the star man. She didn't want to talk about him, much less ask Grandma about him. He was her wonderful secret. Just hers.

★　★　★　★　★

That night she lay awake, staring out of the tiny window in the eaves. When it was pitch dark and the house silent except for Bernie's wheezy breaths, she slipped out of bed, pulled on her jeans, and, with her sneakers in her hand, snuck down the stairs and out of the house. She sat down on the back stoop, pulled on her sneakers, and made her way toward a place where she now knew the fence rail was in ruins.

She could see the star man's outline against the night sky. He was hunched over the telescope in such a way that she could not tell where the man ended and the instrument began. What marvel was he pointing to up there in the sky? The black velvet sky alive with diamonds. Diamonds that were the light from whole systems of worlds millions of miles away, racing through the black emptiness of space for unimaginable years to come to her very own eyes this late-summer night.

Did the stars know about her? Or was she truly nothing—not even a speck of dust—to whatever or whoever was there in those blazing, whirling worlds? *I'm here!* she called out silently. *It's me, Angel Morgan.*

At first, he seemed not to know she was there. She didn't dare speak out. He was still too close to a man from a dream, despite his very real trailer. You didn't interrupt people in dreams; you waited to see what they had to say. Without taking his eye from the eyepiece, he spoke at last. "Did you know that always somewhere out there, there is a new wonder to be seen?"

"No."

He stood up. He had a lit cigarette in his right hand, which he put in his mouth. "There was a time," he said after taking a deep drag and slowly blowing out the smoke, "there was a time I wanted to be the first person in the world to discover something in the sky. People do that, you know. People not so different from me. Just a few years back a man in Essex Junction discovered a nova. He looked for fourteen years. Every clear night for fourteen years." He took the cigarette out of his mouth to cough, a rusty-sounding cough. She wanted to tell him not to smoke, that it wasn't good for him, but she didn't quite dare.

"How old are you, Angel?"

"I'll be twelve next April."

"So fourteen years must seem a long time to you."

"I guess."

"It takes the light from Andromeda two million years to get to earth."

"You told me," she said.

"So that doesn't make fourteen years seem so long, does it?"

"No."

He took another long drag. "I stopped looking after only eight years. Do you know why?"

"No," she said again.

"Because one night I realized I was looking and looking and forgetting to *see*." He propped his cigarette on the little stand between the telescope legs and put his eye on the eyepiece again. "I guess that sounds crazy to you."

"No." In her daytime world it might sound crazy, but not in this enchanted nighttime universe.

"Here," he said, drawing her to the telescope. "Right here, meet Albireo; that's the beak of the swan. They couldn't see it in the old days, but it's really two stars."

The twin stars blinked gold and blue like jewels in a heavenly crown. She wanted to ask him about the swan, since she didn't see anything like a swan in the sky—just jewels. She didn't have to ask, as it turned out.

"Long ago," he began, "people just like you and me looked up at the sky and they began to tell each other stories about what they saw. The stories helped them map the sky." He put one hand upon her shoulder and laid the other lightly against her ear, pointing her gaze away from the eyepiece to the sky itself. "They called that group of six stars Cygnus, which means 'the swan.'"

She nodded, though the cross in the sky above her looked nothing like a bird.

"Albireo is the beak. Deneb, that bright star up there, is the tail. The three stars almost in a line making the breast and wings of the swan are Sadr, Gienah, and Azelfafage."

She giggled, then quickly covered her mouth. She didn't want him to think she was laughing at him.

He went on seriously. "Sadr means 'the breast.' It's the one in the middle. Gienah and Azelfafage mark the wings. And no, I am not sneezing. I'm speaking Arabic. Didn't expect an old broken-down Vermont country boy to speak Arabic, did you?" She knew then that he was smiling, though it was too dark to see his face clearly.

"I was wondering something," she said. His joking had made her bold enough to ask.

"Yeah?"

"Do you think that sometimes they told stories about the stars so they wouldn't be scared? I mean, the universe is so huge, and you look up at the sky and feel so like, well, so like nothing?"

He picked up his cigarette and took another puff. "Could be," he said, and began to cough again.

"Maybe it's not my business." Angel couldn't help herself; she had to say it. "But it's not good for you to smoke. It really isn't."

"No, and it's not good for you to stay up so late listening to an old man carrying on. I'll put out the cigarette, and you get yourself to bed, okay? There'll be other clear nights."

She hated to go, but she went, carrying the heavenly swan inside her. She'd look it up and surprise him by learning the names of the stars. She could remember Albireo. How could she ever forget those twin stars? And Deneb—but the others she'd have to practice. They did sound like sneezes.

Maybe there was a library in the village. She'd ask Grandma, tell her that besides the five basic food groups growing kids needed to read lots of books. If there was a library, she and Bernie could walk there and get books to read. They might have a book about the stars that would be easier to understand than her musty encyclopedia. Bernie wasn't crazy about books. They reminded him too much of school, and he hated school. He'd flunked first grade for spite. He wasn't stupid, just stubborn. Angel would make him go with her to the library, though. Welfare wouldn't separate a little kid from a big sister who made sure he ate right *and* read him lots of books.

At the kitchen door she stopped to take one more look at the sky. She couldn't find the swan. It was though it had flown away and lost itself among the stars.

ELEVEN

Miss Liza of the Library

When Angel and Bernie came downstairs the next morning, there was a brown grocery bag on the kitchen table.

"Where did that come from?" asked Angel. For one wild minute she imagined that Verna had come back in the night.

"It was at the door when I opened it to see what the weather was," Grandma said. "I guess Santy Claus must have brung it."

"Santa Claus don't come in the summertime, Grandma," said Bernie.

"Well, maybe it was the tooth fairy. How should I know?"

"Grandmas aren't supposed to lie to children," Bernie said.

"Oh, be quiet, Bernie. Grandma's just teasing you." Angel didn't care who had brought the bag. She wanted to unload it. Milk, a whole gallon—good. A plastic bag with grapes and some bananas—good. Another box of the cereal Bernie hated, so it couldn't have been Verna who left the groceries. She would know better. A canned ham, not as good-tasting as hamburger but at least another food group, and a loaf of sliced white sandwich bread. Looked like the tooth fairy or Santa Claus or whoever had been boning up on nutrition. There was still "room for improvement," as Ms. Hallingford used to write on report cards, what with the white bread and no vegetables, but they were definitely "showing progress."

"Me, oh my," said Grandma. "I think I'll have me some of that ham for my breakfast. Why don't you open it and fry some up, Angel?"

"I don't like ham," Bernie said.

"Well, who was asking you, junior?"

"I'll just fry up some for Grandma and me. You can have cereal."

"I don't like that kind of cereal. It's yucky."

"Well, it's all we got now. You ate up all the Sugar Pops."

"We can buy some more."

"Not till Grandma gets her check. So what'll it be? Ham or cereal?" Angel went to the sink. The ham had to be opened with the little key that was stuck on the top. She'd watched Verna do it once when there'd been a canned ham in the Salvation Army Christmas basket. She'd never heard Verna cuss as much as she did trying to open that can. Angel pulled the key off and pried up the metal flap. The trick had to be to wind it absolutely straight. "Grandma? Have you ever opened one of these before?"

"Eh-yup."

"Would you mind doing this one?"

"Not on your stuffed cabbage. I tore my hand open last time."

All the time she was talking to Grandma, Bernie was jumping up and down, jabbering, "You not listening to me, Angel!" he said.

"I'm trying to open this can, Bernie. Be quiet."

"I'm starving to death, and you won't give me nothing to eat. Nothing. Nothing. Nothing."

"Shut up, Bernie. There's lots to eat. You're just too picky. That's your problem. If you're starving to death, you eat rats and weeds. That's what really hungry people do."

He began to wail. "I don't want to eat no rats!"

"Well, shut up whining and eat your cereal, then."

He plunked himself on a chair. She left off trying to roll up the metal strip with the phony little key and got him a bowl, filled it with the hated cereal, sprinkled sugar on top, and slopped in milk. "You want a banana with that? We got bananas today."

She knew he wanted a banana, but he kept his mouth in a line and shook his head.

"Okay. You had your chance." She handed him a spoon and went back to winding the key around the can.

"Where's my banana? You said I could have a banana."

The key broke off in her hand, leaving the wretched metal strip less than half pulled off. "Dammit, Bernie, look what you made me do!" Her hands were gucky with the juice seeping out of the partially opened can. "Get your own stupid banana."

"You said a bad word," he muttered, but he got up from his chair and fetched himself a banana.

Now what was she supposed to do? If she tried to take the broken metal strip off the key, she was sure to cut herself to ribbons. There probably wasn't a doctor for miles.

"You could get the pliers out of that bottom drawer and pull it off," Grandma said. "It's a pain, but it'll work if you're careful."

She washed her hands under the faucet. Bernie getting his own banana, Grandma making a smart suggestion—speak of minor miracles. "Thanks," she said to them both, though neither of them acknowledged it.

It *was* a pain, but she finally unwound the strip from the key, pulled it out of the slot, and started winding up the strip still left on the can as slowly and carefully as possible. No one spoke. They all seemed to be holding their breath. "There!" she cried. "I got it."

Grandma clapped her hands. Bernie looked up from his banana, which he was eating monkeylike between bites of cereal. "What's the big deal?" he asked, but he was having to try hard to keep from grinning.

Angel lifted the slimy pink meat out of the can. She had to wash her hands again before she could slice it.

Grandma was well into her second large slice of ham before she said, "Nothing like fried ham for breakfast."

She was talking with her mouth full, but Angel wasn't about to correct her manners. The ham was the best thing she'd had to eat since the hamburger on the way here.

"Ever make gravy?" Grandma asked.

"No." In fact, the only time she could remember having gravy was in a Kentucky Fried place once.

"I think you should learn to make gravy. Me and Bernie would like that."

"You got a cookbook?"

"Aw, you don't learn to cook from a book, girl. You just do it."

Angel sighed. *Then you do it,* she wanted to say. She waited until she'd carefully swallowed her next bite. "I'm just eleven years old, Grandma. Nobody's taught me much about cooking from scratch. I usually just make stuff from boxes. Maybe you could make us some gravy."

"Aw, I ain't really cooked in so long I can't hardly remember how to do it."

"Maybe," Angel said slowly, "maybe the library has cookbooks. There is a library around here somewhere, isn't there?"

"Used to be. That little house next to the store. That used to be a liberry. Maybe still is, if that goody-goody Liza Irwin ain't dead as some might hope." She took a large bite of ham and chomped down on it as if it were the despised Liza. "I ain't been in there myself since I was in grade school. Ain't what you'd call a book lover."

"Me, neither," said Bernie, his mouth so stuffed with

banana that Angel could hardly understand what he was saying.

"Why don't me and Bernie go down and see? I know you don't approve of cooking from a book, but I don't know any other way to learn, and if I'm supposed to give you and Bernie a well-balanced diet, I got to get some help somewhere."

★   ★   ★   ★   ★

Bernie whined all the way, but she half cajoled, half dragged him the two miles to the village center. This time she remembered the taxi money, but she didn't tell him. Better to surprise him with a treat than make a promise that in the end she couldn't keep.

On the green between the store and the church, there was a tiny house. It was set well back from the other buildings, in line with the graveyard, and she hadn't even noticed it the last time they had walked down for groceries. "Come on, Bernie. We got to see if it's open."

"I want to go to the store."

"Maybe, if you're good, we can go after."

"Now."

She ignored him and walked up the path to the little house. Over the door painted in large black letters were the words ELIZABETH FLETCHER IRWIN MEMORIAL LIBRARY. The sign was almost bigger than the building. There was a hand-lettered pasteboard card in the window giving the hours: MON. WED. FRI. 12 NOON TO 3 P.M. Today was Monday—she felt sure about that, but she didn't have a watch so she had no idea if it was noon yet or not. She tried the knob. It turned, and the door opened. They were in luck.

A bell tinkled as they walked in. From the back came a strange little voice. "Make yourself at home. I'll be right out." The witch in Hansel and Gretel! Angel's heart skipped a beat.

She forced a smile at a still belligerent Bernie. "See how friendly they are?" He shrugged. For a minute Angel just stood there barely inside the door, looking around at the shelves of books. It was much tinier than the school library in Burlington, but no use comparing. It was a library. It had books. "You want a book about trucks, Bernie? They probably got a book about trucks." She headed for a sign hanging from the ceiling that said CHILDREN'S.

"No. I hate books about trucks."

"You don't and you know it."

"I do, too. You don't know what I like and what I don't like."

The argument ended abruptly at the sight of a strange, bent-over figure emerging from the curtained doorway in the back wall. "Hello," she said, the curve of her back forcing her to twist her face sideways to look at them as she spoke. Bernie shrank against Angel. She put her arm around his shoulder, willing him to keep his mouth shut.

"I haven't met you before," the woman said. "Are you on vacation here?"

Angel shook her head. "We're visiting our grandma, Miz Morgan, up the road."

"Well, my goodness. I haven't seen Erma Morgan in a hundred years. How is she?"

Surely the woman was teasing about the hundred years. "Fine," said Angel.

"She's more than a hundred years old," Bernie whispered, his eyes wide with shock.

"No, no." The woman laughed a cackly laugh. "I just mean I haven't seen her in a long time. I used to know her back when we were both schoolgirls." She laughed again. "Wa-a-a-y back in the olden days when it was my grandmother, the one I was named after, who ran the library." She rubbed her hands on the apron she was wearing. How did she dress herself in the morning? Angel wondered and tried to picture the little woman pulling clothes over her head and bent back and fastening things. "Now, what can I help you with today?" She may have asked the question more than once while Angel was staring.

Angel's face felt like it was on fire. "I'm a— Grandma thought we might do some cooking while I'm here. And I can't seem to do anything without a book." She laughed apologetically. "So I wonder if you have any cookbooks a kid like me could understand."

"Hmm," said the woman, and she started shuffling toward a shelf to her right. She walked at such an angle that her head got to the place before her feet did.

"What's the matter with her?" Bernie was whispering so loudly that the woman must have heard. If so, she pretended she hadn't.

"Keep your stupid mouth shut for once, Bernie," Angel said in his ear.

The woman turned her whole body around to face them. "Could you give me a hand here, uh—I'm sorry, I didn't get your names—"

"Angel. Angel Morgan. And he's Bernie."

"I'm glad to meet you, Angel, Bernie." She gave a funny little shake of her head in their direction. "Everyone calls me Miss Liza. Now, Angel, if you'd be so kind . . ." Angel left Bernie still standing a few steps from the door and hurried over. Close to the deformed body of the librarian, Angel felt like a giant. Like a giant on the outside, anyway. On the inside she was feeling, well, as though she wanted to reach out her hand and touch the strange little woman's wrinkled cheek. *She knows how it feels to have everyone staring at her and whispering behind her back, but it hasn't made her mean. It hasn't even made her pull into a shell.*

"I have some tongs here somewhere, but why don't you just reach up"—the librarian waved her crooked arm toward the top shelf—"and see if you can find what you're looking for." She swiveled her head from one side to the other. "There's a stool around here, I know."

Angel located the stool and climbed up to survey the shelf. There were at least a half-dozen cookbooks. She looked at the titles carefully. *Cooking Made Easy*. That should do it. She pulled it out. It must have been bought by the librarian's grandmother. The pages were almost yellow. There were no pictures, and the print was teeny. She put it back. One by one she examined all the books. She could feel Bernie's fear from across the room. "I'm sorry to be so slow. . . . It's just—"

"No, no," Miss Liza said. "Take all the time you need. Meanwhile—Bernie, is it? Would you like to see some books?"

Angel waited for Bernie's "No," but it didn't come. He was probably still frozen witless. "Go on, Bernie." She turned from the cookbooks. "Get yourself something to look at. I'm going to be a while."

"How about if I read you a story?" the little old lady asked. "What kind of story would you like?"

Still no answer from Bernie. "He likes trucks," Angel called.

"I do not!" said Bernie. "Trucks are stupid. Stupid. Stupid. Stupid."

"I know just the story for you, Bernie Morgan," the librarian said.

Soon Angel could hear Miss Liza's voice reading: "'One day Stanley Q. Stupid had an idea. This was unusual. "Calling all Stupids!" Stanley shouted.'"

"Why are they all stupid?" Bernie asked.

"That's their name," said Miss Liza. "Mr. Stanley Q. Stupid, his wife, Mrs. Stupid, Buster Stupid, Petunia

Stupid, and their wonderful dog called— Can you guess what they call their dog, Bernie?"

"Stupid!"

"No, they call their dog Kitty."

"Kitty Stupid!" said Bernie, and he laughed right out loud.

Angel snatched the newest-looking of the cookbooks off the shelf and hurried over to hear the story of the Stupids, who tried to slide up the banisters and take baths with no water, for fear they'd wet their clothes. Mrs. Stupid perched a cat on her head instead of a hat, and Mr. Stupid wore his new socks on his ears. When Bernie saw that picture, he shrieked with laughter. And by the time the Stupids ate their mashed-potato sundaes with butterscotch syrup he was almost rolling on the floor.

"It's my guess," said Miss Liza, "that you like the Stupids. You might want to know that we have more books by Harry Allard and James Marshall." She got up from the child-sized chair she had been sitting on and found Bernie another book. She twisted her face up toward Angel. "And what kind of book would you like, Angel? In addition to your cookbook?"

"Do you—um—do you have one about stars?" Angel asked.

Miss Liza smiled, looking nothing at all like a witch. "Ah," she said, almost to herself. "I think we must have a mutual friend."

That meant the librarian knew the star man. It only

seemed right that she should, both of them being so different from ordinary people. Angel longed to ask the librarian about him, but something kept her quiet. What sort of questions were you supposed to ask about a man you only saw on starry nights and who told you so little about himself?

Miss Liza took a small paperback book from a nearby shelf. Angel caught a glimpse of the title: *Know the Stars.* Good. That was what she wanted—to know the stars. The librarian sat down at the desk and printed their names and "Morgan Farm Road" on cards. "You may keep your books for two weeks," she said.

"We can't come back for two whole weeks?" Bernie cried.

"No, no, you can come anytime you want," she said, handing him his books, which he clutched to his chest as though afraid she would change her mind about lending them out. "Don't pay any attention to the sign. I'm nearly always here. Just knock hard if the door is locked. It hardly ever is."

Bernie was so tickled when they left the library that Angel had forgotten about the treat. Bernie hadn't. "I need a Popsicle," he said when they were in front of the store.

"Me, too," said Angel.

Walking home, carrying their library books under one arm, licking a Fudgsicle, she didn't even mention to Bernie that his Popsicle was dripping down his shirt front.

"Mashed-potato sundaes!" Bernie exclaimed suddenly.

"With butterscotch syrup!" Angel answered. They both nearly collapsed on the road, they were giggling so hard.

"Grandma! Grandma!" Bernie yelled, racing into the house ahead of Angel. "I got a book all about Stupids. Everybody in the book is stupid."

"Yeah?" Grandma was in her rocker. "That's all we need around here—more stupidity. Well," she said to Angel, "I take it she ain't dead yet."

"Who?"

"Liza Irwin. Who do you think?"

"She's a hundred years old!" Bernie said. "And she's all crooked like her back broke over."

"Hmmph," said Grandma, a little smile playing around her lips. "Even uglier than me, huh?"

"But I wasn't scared of her one bit," Bernie went on. "She's nice."

The smile deserted Grandma's face. "So I guess now you like her better than you do me, huh? Well, why don't you just go live at her house, then. Go on. See if I care."

Bernie looked stricken. "I didn't mean I wanted to live with her. I just mean I like the Stupids."

"Then you better stay with me. Being stupid was the only thing I could ever beat that smart little Liza Irwin at."

Angel wanted to say something, but what? *Don't be so down on yourself, Grandma. You're really smart!* Or *C'mon,*

Grandma, Bernie and me think you're just fine. While she stood there, not knowing what to say or do, Bernie went over to the rocker and put his arm around the thin shoulders. "Don't worry, Grandma. Angel and me likes you the best, and we always will. Always. Always. Always." He had his anxious little face right up in her old wrinkled one. "Okay?"

"Hmmph," she said.

A shrill sound pierced the quiet, making Angel jump. Another shriek. Another. The phone. The phone was ringing. She ran to snatch it off the hook. "Hello?"

"Would you accept a collect call from Wayne Morgan?"

"Yeah. Yes. Sure," Angel said. She'd give Grandma the rest of her taxi money. She needed to talk to Daddy. She really did.

TWELVE

Know the Stars

"Daddy? Hi, it's me, Angel." She was keeping her voice low, so as not to get Grandma upset.

"What's the matter, baby?" Wayne's voice sounded pinched, like Bernie's when he was scared. "I tried to call you back soon's I got your message, but whoever answered wouldn't take the call."

"I don't want to worry you, Daddy. Me and Bernie are okay, but we're not in Burlington anymore." Angel sneaked a glance at Grandma. Bernie was showing her the Stupids book and poking her, trying to make her laugh at the pictures. Angel cupped her hand around the mouthpiece. "We're at your grandma's house."

"You're where? At *Grandma's*? Well, where the hell's Verna?"

"That's what I'm calling about, Daddy. Remember when we came to see you? Well, she brought us here that day. Then she left, and she hasn't come back."

"Well, where's she at, then? Did you call the apartment?"

"The phone's been disconnected."

She could hear him curse under his breath. "Jeez—

just dumped you kids there with that old witch and took off?"

"I don't think she meant to—"

Grandma looked up from the book. "Who's on the phone?"

"It's Daddy." That "not on your stuffed cabbage" look began to creep onto Grandma's face, so Angel hurried on. "I'll pay for the call, promise."

Grandma muttered something, but she didn't say "Hang up," so Angel turned back to the phone. "I thought you ought to know where me and Bernie moved to."

"I don't understand what's got into her. I told her there's a good chance I might get put on an outside work crew, and she just takes off. I swear I could kill that girl!"

"No, no, Daddy. Don't blame Verna. She's been under a lot of stress." Angel tried to go around the corner, but the phone cord was too short. It kept her smack in the doorway.

"*She's* been under a lotta stress! She should trying sitting in the stir for a few years if she thinks she knows anything about stress. Judas Priest!"

"I guess you don't know where she's at, then?"

"I wish I did, baby doll, I just wish I did. I'd get the law after her faster than you could say 'child neglect.'"

"Oh, Daddy, please. Don't tell anyone she's gone. They'd send Welfare out here and take us away."

"Well, how are you kids going to stay with that old bat? She near ran me crazy when I was a kid, and that was years ago. You can't tell me she's improved none with age. You and Bernie'd be better off if Welfare did come and get you."

"No, we *wouldn't*." Why had she been so bent on talking to Wayne? "No, we *wouldn't*. Don't you see, Daddy, they'd separate us, and who would take care of Bernie then?"

"I swear. Verna must be out of her cotton-picking head—dumping *my* son and *my* daughter on the very woman I hate the most in the frigging world. I get in the least little trouble, and my own grandma throws me *and* my whole family out of her stinking trailer. She's probably the one sicced the cops on me, the old witch. I know she's the one turned my daddy in and run my mama off. I swear I'm calling Welfare."

"Daddy. *Daddy!* Don't call anybody. Please. We're okay, really we are. Besides, I can take care of Bernie. He's behaving himself real good right now. Okay? Don't worry about us, okay?" The frantic whispering was making her throat raw. "Okay? You just take care of yourself. Bernie and me will be *fine*. I promise. Bye, now." She hung up the phone, hoarse and wet with perspiration. That would teach her to use up all her money to make a stupid long-distance call.

Angel turned from the phone to see that Grandma was directing her full attention at her. "So?" the old woman said.

"He doesn't know where Verna is, either."

Grandma snorted. "I figure that rascal'd be the last person on earth she'd want to know her whereabouts."

Angel sighed and slumped down on one of the kitchen chairs. "I was just hoping—"

"If I was you, Angel, I'd pour my hopes into some other bucket. Those two are leaky as sieves." Grandma was in a good mood again. It was almost as if other people's failures and misfortunes cheered her up. "Now," she said, "how about you fixing us up some nice fat ham sandwiches for lunch?"

"I hate ham," said Bernie, but when Angel made a sandwich for him he ate it with hardly a whimper.

★　★　★　★　★

It was cloudy that night. No use going out to look for the star man. She waited until Bernie was asleep, then took her library book across the hall. No use looking for Verna, either. Angel pulled on the overhead light. It was another naked bulb hanging down from the ceiling, so dim she'd probably put her eyes out, but never mind. She stretched out on the bed and opened the worn paperback called *Know the Stars*. "Few people," it began, "can tell one star from another, yet it is not difficult to know them. . . ."

Angel blinked at the wonderful first sentence. She was ignorant, but she was not alone. The writer of this book, H. A. Rey, thought she could learn, not like the guy who wrote the encyclopedia article, who thought she had to know everything first before she could understand anything. The writer went on: "Simple shepherds 5000 years ago were familiar with the heavens; they knew the stars and constellations—and they could not even read or write—so why don't you?"

A feeling totally unknown to her flooded her with warmth. Maybe it was what some people called "love at first sight." She loved this writer. She loved his book. He knew her and he didn't sneer. He was going to help her. There were lots of pictures that the writer had drawn himself. He loved the night sky and he was going to teach her all about it. Between H. A. Rey and the star man, she was going to delve into a realm of mystery so huge that the disappearance of Verna Morgan would look like nothing. Wouldn't it?

★   ★   ★   ★   ★

The cookbook choice had been a mistake, for when she tried to follow the directions it gave for making gravy, it didn't work. It wanted her to use fancy ingredients that she didn't have, like steak sauce and a special kind of flour. The only flour in Grandma's house had little meal-worms crawling about in it. Even when Angel tried her best to pick them out and use the flour anyway, the gravy she made turned out tasteless and lumpy. Maybe Miss Liza knew how to make gravy, but if she went back to the library, she'd have to return *Know the Stars,* and she needed its explanations and pictures with the dotted lines to make sense of the constellations.

She had wanted to surprise the star man by pointing out the Big Bear with the Big Dipper riding like a saddle on its back. But when she looked at the real sky, which didn't have any dotted lines connecting stars into constellations, she couldn't even find the Little Dipper with Polaris, the North Star, at the end of its handle. Polaris was practically the most important star in the whole sky, and she had pointed at Venus and said it was Polaris.

"Don't worry," the star man had said. "It's hard for everyone at first."

She would have given up without H. A. Rey and the star man. They both thought she could learn the map of the sky, but she'd need Mr. Rey's book for longer than two weeks, that was for sure. Besides, the sky was changing all the time. When fall came, everything would be different. It was already getting dark sooner, which was good for looking at the sky but a reminder that she had to think of other things—mostly, school. If only she and Bernie could just not go. But if they didn't go, Welfare was sure to find out, and then they wouldn't have a prayer of staying here with Grandma and the star man.

Angel didn't have any idea what day school began, but August was more than half over. It was bound to begin soon. She'd just have to ask Miss Liza. That was it. As soon as the blinking check came, she'd have to go to the village.

Grandma sent Angel to the mailbox every day. "It ain't ever been this late," she'd say. When it came at last, Grandma signed the back with a shaky hand. Now they could go to the store and get food in all five food groups instead of getting by on what Santy Claus left on their doorstep.

"What did you do before?" Angel asked Grandma.

"What do you mean, 'before'?"

"I mean, who cashed your check and brought you groceries before me and Bernie came?"

"Santy Claus."

It was no use. Maybe the star man had done that, too. By now, Angel had figured that it was probably the star man who left the occasional bag of groceries at the door and cut and stacked the wood in the pile next to the house. She wondered how he knew they needed help. He might as well have been Grandma's Santy Claus. He was as hard to believe in, a mysterious figure of the night. Angel refused to let herself think of him in earthbound terms, even though in one part of her mind she knew he lived in a broken-down trailer and seemed to go to work every day in a rusted-out car. And she wasn't going to ask Grandma about him and have the old woman sneer and call him Santy Claus. Of course, she could have asked the star man about school, but she didn't want to. She didn't want him connected to anything so ordinary as school.

★　★　★　★　★

Funny, she was nervous about seeing the librarian again. The books were only one day overdue. Still, nice as Miss Liza might seem, she was a librarian, and librarians could be very fussy about getting books back on time.

"I don't want to take my books back," Bernie said.

"You have to. They're overdue."

"I don't care. I'm never taking them back. Never. Never. Never."

Angel sighed. She would have yelled if she hadn't been so sympathetic. "Maybe Miss Liza will find you some other books. She said she would."

"I like these."

It was all Angel could do to put Bernie's shoes on him, wrestle the Stupids out of his hands, and drag him out the door and down the road. He complained all the way, but she paid him no attention. She was making the list in her head of things to ask Miss Liza. Could she renew *Know the Stars* even if she was bringing it back late? Would Miss Liza find her a better cookbook with no fancy ingredients? When did school start? And where was it? She plotted her strategy. First they'd go to the library, get things straight with Miss Liza, and then they'd go to the store. It was a big check—three hundred sixty-four dollars. She could buy only what she and Bernie could carry between them, but the idea of carrying that much money scared her. This was what you needed grownups for—these kinds of things. Every time she thought about it, she got mad.

The door to the library was unlocked, just as if Miss Liza were expecting them. The bell rang when they pushed the door open. "Come on in!" Miss Liza's crackly voice called from the back. "Make yourself at home. I'll be right out."

Bernie zoomed across to the picture books. He knew

right where Miss Liza had found the Stupids, and before she emerged from the back, he had settled down happily on the floor, books strewn all around him.

Miss Liza shuffled in, reminding Angel less of a witch than of a crab, coming with her head sideways so she could see something besides the floor. "My favorite people!" she exclaimed. "Angel and Bernie!"

"I need some more Stupids!" Bernie said. He jumped up and ran to her, grabbing her clawed hand to lead her to the picture books.

"Looks to me like you already found them," she said, her eyes wrinkled up in smiles. "And what about you, Miss Angel? What do you need today?"

"I was wondering—I know everything's overdue, but, well, would it be okay if I renew the star book?"

"Keep it as long as you need to," Miss Liza said. "If someone else comes in wanting to borrow it, I'll let you know. All right?"

"Yes, ma'am." They smiled at each other, Angel realizing at once that the likelihood of someone else wanting that particular book was very slim.

"How about the cookbook? Was it any help?"

"Well, it wants you to have stuff we don't have."

"So, something simpler that doesn't call for fancy ingredients?"

Angel nodded.

"Hmm. Let me think." She didn't go to the cookbook section but to a part of the children's section and brought out a paperback book that had a spiral binding. "Here's one the 4-H Club put out with someone just like you in mind." She handed the book over to Angel. "I should have thought of it last time."

"Thanks. And I got another question. It—it looks like we're going to be at Grandma's longer than we first thought. Mama thinks we ought to go ahead and start school." She looked over at Bernie to see if he was going to say anything, but he was happily leafing through a Stupids book. "She wanted me to find out when school starts around here."

"Well, that's an easy one. A week from today, the day after Labor Day."

"I'm sure Mama knows, but Bernie and me was curious as to where the school building is. I mean, do we walk, or take a bus, or what?"

"I'm afraid they closed down the school here in the village a few years ago. Tell your mama"—she looked closely at Angel as she said the word, as though she was suspicious about Mama but too polite to question—"I'm sure your mama remembers that the school's in Chesterville now." Miss Liza sidled over to the desk, opened a drawer, and pulled out a thin yellow phone book. "I'll write down the number of the school for you. Then they can tell you where to catch the bus, that sort of thing."

"Thank you. C'mon, Bernie." Bernie stooped down and began picking up every book he'd yanked from shelves earlier. When he stood up, books were falling out from under both his arms. "You can't take more than two. We still got to carry the groceries." He started to argue but sighed instead. After a long time of examining every book, he carefully chose the same two books he'd taken home the time before. She opened her mouth to suggest that he might want a new one, but Miss Liza shot her a warning glance. "I thought you didn't like books," Angel said.

"I don't," he said. "I only like Stupids."

Miss Liza stamped the cards and handed them their books. Then she leaned down in her dangerous way that made Angel fear she'd topple over, and pulled something out of the bottom drawer. It was an almost new–looking canvas backpack. "Somebody left this here two or three years ago," she said, pushing it across the desk toward Angel. "Why don't you take it? It might come in handy."

A real backpack! She wouldn't be so weird at school if she had a backpack like everyone else. "Are you sure it's okay if I take it?"

"Positive," Miss Liza said. "And if you have any problems, with school or anything else, call me. All right, Angel?"

"Thank you. I'll, I'll tell Mama you offered." Nobody in town, even somebody as nice as Miss Liza, could know that Mama was missing. Sometimes the people with the kindest hearts caused the worst trouble for kids.

Angel planned the next steps carefully. First she

cashed Grandma's check and bought each of them a Popsicle. "We'll be right back to get groceries," she explained to the clerk. "We got to eat these first."

"Suit yourself," the woman said.

They sat on the steps of the store and ate the Popsicles. "Bernie, you can't look at your book and eat your Popsicle at the same time. You'll drip all over it," Angel said.

"You are so mean." But she knew he didn't mean it.

She stretched out her feet in dirty sneakers with no socks. The sun was warm on her bare ankles. A fly buzzing over a drop of melted Popsicle that had dripped on the step was the loudest noise to be heard in the late-summer morning. She licked contentedly. "This is great, isn't it, Bernie?"

"I wanted grape," he said.

"Well, you should have said so, Bernie. I asked, and you said 'orange' plain as day. I can't read your blinking mind."

"I know," he said happily.

Everything was going to be all right. Oh, they had parents that acted like spoiled babies and a great-grandma who needed a mother as much as they did, and in this immense universe they weren't even specks of dust, but somehow, somehow, they were going to make it. She knew it, sitting on those steps eating a cherry Popsicle, a real backpack on her back with books inside waiting to be read, and groceries in all five major food groups waiting to be bought. She didn't have anything to worry about today, and she wasn't going to get all stressed out about tomorrow. Not while she had the chill syrupy taste of a cherry Popsicle in her mouth.

THIRTEEN

To School We Go

She put off calling the school. She even asked Grandma to do it. "Not on your stuffed cabbage," the old lady said. "I don't mess with the authorities." Angel practiced deepening her voice in her chest, saying things like, "This is Mrs. Verna Morgan. I intend to enroll my children in your school." Or "Excuse me, please, but where does the school bus stop on Morgan Farm Road?" But even in her own head she sounded like a kid playing grownup. So she gave up trying to imitate Verna and just called. The school phone was busy. It stayed busy. She'd almost lost her nerve and decided to forget about school when suddenly there was a long ring at the other end and a voice barked, "Chesterville Union Elementary School."

"Uh—"

"Yeah, what is it?"

"I need to know about where the bus stops."

She could hear a sigh at the other end. "Honey, the buses stop all over the district. You got to pick a spot."

"On—on Morgan Farm Road."

"Wait a minute. I got to check the map." She came

back after what seemed to Angel halfway to forever. "No stops on that road. No kids."

"Yes, there are. Me and my brother. We just moved here . . . my mom, too, only she's real busy right now and can't come to the phone. Or else she'd be—"

"Okay. Okay. Where do you live?"

"Well, my mother and my brother and me are living with my grandmother, my *great*-grandmother. For right now."

The voice got very stiff, like somebody had told the woman to practice being patient with slow learners and she didn't like having to do it. "I don't know your *great*-grandmother, honey. So you need to tell me who she is and where she's at."

"She's Mrs. Morgan. Mrs. Erma Morgan. The same as the road. I don't think there's any number—"

"Hold on a minute, okay?" Angel could hear the woman conferring with somebody else. "Okay. Looks like it'll have to be a new stop. The bus will stop right by your mailbox. Now, that will be the elementary school bus, won't it?"

"There's more than one bus?"

Another sigh. "Honey, we got five different schedules to coordinate. Kindergarten. That's morning *and* afternoon. Elementary. That's one through five. Middle school, which, in case you're wondering, is six through eight. And high school. But I'm guessing you don't need to know about that last one."

Angel felt panicky all over. She'd never imagined that

she and Bernie would be riding different buses. What would he do if she wasn't with him?

"Now, which bus was it?"

"I don't know—I mean—"

"This is a busy day, honey. Could you get your mother to call later? I could explain everything to her."

Angel hung up the phone.

Grandma was watching her from the rocker. "See what I mean? They treat you like scum on a frog pond. I bet they didn't even tell you what time the dang thing went past here."

"Grandma, it's two different buses."

"Two?"

"Yeah. I got to ride one and Bernie has to ride a whole 'nother one."

"Well, you didn't expect them to make it simple for you, now, did you?"

"What am I going to do?" She was talking to herself. She wasn't asking for help.

"Well, you could try not going a-tall. By the time I was your age—"

"Welfare would be after me and Bernie for sure then."

"And why do them snoops have to know where you're at?"

"I already told the woman at the school where we live, Grandma."

She shook her head sadly. "And I thought you was so smart."

"Do you know the telephone number for the library?"

Grandma bristled. "Just what does that Liza Irwin have to do with anything?"

"Well, I need a grownup to call the school and find out about the schedules. They don't want to talk to a kid. Of course . . ." She came over and knelt beside the rocking chair. "They'd pay attention to you if you called them."

"Are you trying to fancy-talk me?"

"Not on your stuffed cabbage, Grandma."

Grandma rose to her feet. "Hmmph. Get me that number."

Another series of busy signals until at last she got through once more to the grumpy secretary, who did talk to Grandma. It was worse than Angel had imagined. Bernie's bus would come forty-five minutes *after* Angel's. He'd never go to school without her policing him. Besides, she couldn't have him standing out there on the road by himself. No telling what would happen.

"Oh, Grandma, what'll I do?"

Grandma sighed, headed back for her chair, and plumped herself down. Finally, she said in a tired voice, "I reckon I'll have to walk him down."

"You?"

The old woman pulled up her skirt, raised her legs, and stared at them. "Spindly, but they ain't broke yet. I s'pose next thing I know you'll be telling me I oughta go all the way to school with him the first day."

"Oh, Grandma, would you? That would be so great!" Angel could feel the cares rolling off her shoulders like water off a dish drain. Grandma *was* going to help. She was. She was. She wouldn't have to do everything for herself and Bernie. Grandma would help. She wanted to kiss the old woman right on the face, but she was too shy. There was no telling how Grandma would react to kissing.

★   ★   ★   ★   ★

Getting through the first day at a new school was worse than visiting the jail, but like the jail visits, she'd had plenty of practice. This was her eighth school in six years. Verna never could stay in one place very long, and besides all the moving they did with Verna, there were the two terms in foster care. No wonder she was always thinking about things Ms. Hallingford said. She had been Angel's teacher for a whole year. No one else had taught Angel more than a few weeks or months.

In the middle school office, Angel was given all sorts of papers to take home and have her mother sign. She'd just get Grandma to do it—or sign Verna's name herself. She'd done that often enough in the past. They hardly ever questioned it.

She didn't want to use any of Grandma's check money for lunch, so she'd brought a peanut butter sandwich for herself. It stuck to the roof of her mouth like tar. She longed for milk or juice or something to wash it down, but she felt embarrassed getting up and going to drink from the water fountain every few bites.

It was confusing changing to different rooms for different classes, but everybody was in the same boat. This was everyone's first year at the middle school, and even if some of the kids pretended to know their way around, she could see in the way their eyes shifted, looking for room numbers, and from the high-pitched yelling and giggling that most of them were nearly as nervous as she was.

No one spoke to her in the cafeteria. Everyone seemed to have friends from the year before to eat with. She caught one girl staring at her. When she stared back, the girl looked away, and began talking to someone close by.

I don't want friends, she told herself. *Friends get nosy. I don't want to have to explain about Verna. How could I anyway? Or about Wayne.* Her heart sank when she thought of him back in Burlington with no one to visit, no one to care whether he lived or died. Nobody deserved that kind of life, did they? No matter what they had done. Everyone needed somebody to care about them. Even Grandma, who probably thought she didn't. But today Grandma was taking Bernie to school. *Oh, mercy, let it go okay. Let Bernie behave himself. And while you're at it, God, let Grandma behave herself.*

"You just moved here, didn't you?" The girl whom she'd caught staring a few minutes before had come over to her table. She was in new jeans and a bright-red turtleneck shirt that was stretched tight across her already developing breasts. Her brown hair was curly and framed her face. With a pang, Angel realized that here was a girl somebody cared enough about that they'd bought her new clothes and taken her to a beauty parlor for the first day of school. She pushed her own hair off her face.

"I'm Megan Armstrong," the girl said. "Who are you?"

"What's it to you?" The words just popped out.

"Okay, okay," said Megan, walking away. "We were just wondering who you were." She went back to her friends to report. They all looked quickly at Angel and then began talking and giggling behind their hands.

She didn't care. She really didn't. All she had to do was get through the wretched day. The first day was always the worst, and sometimes after a week or so she could spot someone else who was on the edge of things, some other kid who didn't want to talk about home, who just wanted somebody to eat lunch with so as not to stick out so much. It might take a while, but she could wait. She always had before. At one of the schools she'd gone to, it took three months before anyone knew her dad was in prison. That was a record. Someone usually found out in a few weeks. She could tell when it had happened because her lunch partner was suddenly no longer at the accustomed table. At her last school a girl named Chantille Saunders's father was in jail, too. So even if neither of them wanted to talk about it, they ate their free lunches together until school let out. Come to think of it, if Bernie hadn't been such a problem in first grade, last year in Ms. Hallingford's class would have been her all-time best school year.

But, as they say, that was then, this was now. She wondered what would happen if she jumped up on the lunchroom table and yelled out to everyone: "Hey, you losers. My daddy's in jail. Want to make something of it?" What would Megan Armstrong and her fancy friends think then? They were curious about her or they wouldn't have sent Megan over, but what would they do if they knew who she really was? *Scum on a frog pond.* Being a Morgan from Morgan Farm Road wasn't as great a thing as she'd first thought. Well, she didn't care. All she wanted was for Bernie to get through the day okay. If it was all right for Bernie, she could stand anything.

No one except teachers spoke to her for the rest of the day. In each new class she tried to find a desk in the back corner of the classroom, where she could hunch into herself and just stare at backs of people's heads without them looking at her. When she'd gone to the office first thing, she'd been given a schedule to follow, but of course none of the teachers had her on their rolls, so she had to give her name and address again each time—language arts, science, social studies, math, gym (no, she didn't have any other sneakers and hadn't brought shorts and an extra T-shirt), and a class that for the next nine weeks was something called library skills, but later in the year would be either art or music. At first, she was disappointed—she'd rather hoped for art—except that Mrs. Coates, the librarian, seemed really nice, almost as nice as Miss Liza, with a library twice as big.

No, she had no report card from her previous school, but, yes, she did know the name of the school. She supposed they would have to call and get her health and academic records. *Health records!* She'd forgotten that Bernie would need those as well. She'd have to persuade Grandma to call about them. Grandma wouldn't know the name of his previous school, and Bernie would probably refuse to tell. He didn't exactly leave North Burlington Elementary with a shining reputation. *Oh Lord, is he behaving himself?* The elementary school building was right next to the middle school, but it might as well have been light-years away. She'd never see him during the day, never be able to listen to his complaints, never be able to remind him to behave.

She couldn't worry about Bernie now. She had to get through the day. She'd managed to scrounge up a pencil and a few sheets of paper, but this afternoon she'd have to go down to the store and get a proper notebook and a pack of lined paper. All the other kids seemed to have notebooks with movie scenes on the covers, little calculators, ballpoint pens, and lots of sharp pencils with pink erasers that no one had ever used, much less chewed on, but Angel didn't waste envy on them. She knew she couldn't afford those things.

Except for the brief encounter with Megan in the cafeteria, she was able to get through the day without anyone paying much attention to her. Even on the bus, she got a seat by herself, and the driver remembered without asking where to drop her off.

The house was empty. How could that be? She'd expected to walk in and find Grandma rocking away, ready to report how everything had gone. "Grandma? Grandma!" It was spooky to walk in and hear her own voice echo in the empty kitchen. She knocked gently on Grandma's door. Maybe she was taking a nap. When there was no answer, she turned the knob and peered in. No Grandma, but that didn't mean the room was empty. It was jammed with cardboard boxes and stacks of newspapers and magazines—a worse jumble than the sugar shack. You could hardly see the bed or the dresser for the mess. A fire hazard, plain and simple. If Welfare showed up, the sight of that room alone would make them snatch her and Bernie away. She closed the door quickly. She didn't want Grandma to pop up out of nowhere and catch her snooping.

She looked up at the kitchen clock. It was two fifty-five. Bernie's bus was due at three forty-five. She didn't know what to do with herself until then. It occurred to her later that she should have enjoyed the peaceful patch of time, read her book, taken a nap, but all she could do was pace up and down the worn kitchen linoleum and keep willing the hands on the clock to move faster. *Has Grandma disappeared like Verna?* Was she so sick and tired of Angel and Bernie that she'd just run away from home? Where on earth could she be? Angel should never have made her think she had to look after Bernie. That was it. The last straw. *But I couldn't help it. He had to have someone to watch him at the bus stop. And she offered. I didn't force her into it. She said she would.*

At three thirty, she couldn't stand it any longer and ran down to the mailbox, only to start pacing up and down the road, craning for a sight of the yellow bus. *Oh Lord, how am I going to explain about Grandma to Bernie?*

She heard the bus before she saw it, shifting gears to get up the hill on the far side of the trailer. Finally, it lumbered into view, coming bumpily down the middle of the dirt road. With a squeal of brakes and flashing of lights, it pulled up by the mailbox.

The door whooshed open. "Okay, kids, hop on it. I ain't got all day."

Kids? What did the driver mean, *kids*?

She soon saw. First, Bernie bounced down the stairs, then slowly, very slowly, clinging to the rail as long as possible, Grandma. As soon as she was on the ground, the driver yanked the door shut.

"Grandma?"

"Well, I couldn't call a taxi now, could I?"

"She stayed in my room all day!" Bernie was practically jumping up and down. "I was the only kid at school with a grandma in my class all day!"

"Are you okay, Grandma?" Angel asked anxiously. The old woman's lined face was not nearly so cheery as Bernie's round one.

"Ah, ginger snaps!" the old woman exclaimed. "Let's get in there and get us something to eat. Have you ever tried to eat that pig slop in the school lunchroom? *Bleeeh.*"

Bernie giggled with delight. "Me and Grandma throwed our whole lunch in the garbitch!"

"Oh, *Bernie.*" Well, anyway he was happy. It couldn't have gone too badly.

She gave Grandma some warmed-over coffee and a piece of toast and made a peanut butter and jelly sandwich with milk for Bernie. The milk looked so cool and inviting, she poured herself a glass and drank it quickly, feeling guilty about downing milk she ought to save for Bernie.

"You need any school supplies, Bernie? I got to run to the store and get me some."

Bernie looked at Grandma. Did he expect her to remember what he was supposed to bring the next day? "Nah," said Grandma. "They got more junk in that room than they know what to do with now. We ain't spending our Social Security check for none, are we, Bernie boy?"

"Nah." They both began to giggle.

Angel cleared her throat. "I'm sorry, Grandma, but I'm going to have to borrow some of your money. Verna will pay you back later." The old woman snorted in disbelief, but what else could Angel do? She'd given Grandma all the rest of her taxi money for the phone calls, and she had to have the supplies. "You want to walk to the store with me, Bernie?"

"Nah. I'm too tired. Me and Grandma need to rest, right, Grandma?"

She was relieved, really. She could go so much faster without him, and she wouldn't have to use even more money to buy him a treat. But as she walked down the road, she kicked the dust. He had always depended on her up until now. He'd always chosen to be with her over anybody else around. She almost felt like crying.

FOURTEEN

Draco the Dragon

If it hadn't been for the stars, she might have given up trying. Going to school was like running through a minefield in a war movie. She had to keep up the lie that her mother was home but the doctor had ordered her to bed because of severe back trouble, so she wasn't able to take phone calls or to come in for a conference. She avoided all the other kids like poison. That was the easy part. No one was dying to be buddies with her.

She tried not to let it rub her raw that Bernie and Grandma were thick as thieves and treated her like she was some stern parent when she tried to make them eat their vegetables or practice reading—Bernie, that is. She didn't try to make Grandma read, but Grandma was no help with Bernie. She just giggled and acted silly when Angel was trying to help him, which made him all silly, too.

So she couldn't have stood it without the nights of starry skies. She would wait until Bernie and Grandma were asleep, pinching herself to stay awake, no matter how tired she was, and then sneak out to the old pasture. The star man was always there before her, lost in the heavens. She would wait beside him quietly, not daring to disturb him, until suddenly he would begin talking about the sky.

"There's old Draco the Dragon, his tail slinking around, dividing the Big Bear from his little brother. Want to see?" Then he'd adjust the telescope to her height and let her look. When she would squint and squint and still not be able to see what he was talking about, he would make her look at the naked sky and point out the constellation. "Okay. Find Dubhe in the lip of the Big Dipper and look toward the North Star—Polaris." She obeyed. "Now, the tip of the dragon's tail is just between Dubhe and Polaris. Then it snakes around and takes a sharp bend"—he drew it in the air with his pointed finger— "and ends in another sort of dipper. That's the dragon's head. See the bright star at the end of its snout and the star beside it? In ancient times those were called the dragon's eyes. But the beautiful double star is on the top of its head. You need to see that through the telescope." And then, with unbelievable patience, he would help her find the pair of beautiful pale-yellow stars in Draco's head.

Angel could not remember it all, of course. She would go back to bed and lie there in the dark, head spinning, too tired to look up anything in her beloved book, too excited to sleep. It had taken more years than she could conceive of for the light from those stars to reach her eye. To her they were the most magnificent, the most wonderful, things she had ever seen. When the stars sent that light rushing toward the earth, she, Angel Morgan, wasn't even alive, wasn't even going to be *born* for ages and ages. She shivered. To the stars she was not even pond scum. Not even a speck of dust. Not even . . . not even . . . She tried to think of something smaller than nothing, but she couldn't imagine it.

★ ★ ★ ★ ★

Three weeks after school began, Megan Armstrong, who hadn't spoken to her since the first day of school, came strolling over to where Angel sat eating her peanut butter and jelly sandwich in the back corner of the lunchroom. "It isn't true, is it?" she said in a snooty sort of voice.

It took a few seconds for Angel, who had been lost in the stars, to realize that Megan was talking to her. "Huh?"

"It isn't true that your father is the Wayne Morgan who robbed the Cumberland Farms in Barre a few years ago?"

"I don't know what you're talking about." Angel wasn't faking. She really didn't know what Wayne had or had not done. Nobody had ever said.

Megan gave a twisted smile and sniffed. "Just wondering," she said. "It was in the papers a while back. The guy was sent to jail . . . for a long time." She studied Angel's face, which Angel willed to be blank. Finally, Megan turned away. Angel watched her go back to her usual table to report.

So the word was out. Somebody's mom or dad or grandparent had a long memory. Vermont was a small state. Morgans were known around here, for good or bad.

It had taken just three weeks. The girls were whispering and giggling and stealing glances at her. She stared back. She wasn't going to let them think they could humiliate her. How many of them knew that the star Rigel was 545 light-years from earth? They probably didn't even know what a light-year was. Or that to the stars at the farthest rim of the universe they weren't even going to be born for billions of years. They weren't anything more than she was. Less than pond scum, less than dust, less than nothing at all.

Still, she wished they hadn't found out quite so soon. Before, she was nothing in their eyes, but now, though still less than nothing, she was as visible as the sun. Which she bet they didn't know was 93 million miles away—the closest star. Which was a fiery ball that would burn you up if you got too close. She put all of Megan's gang into a spaceship and shot them straight at the sun.

Somehow she got through the day, trying hard to ignore the fact that all conversations stopped abruptly when she walked past, as eyes sidled toward her. It wasn't as if it hadn't happened before. She ought to be used to it by now, shouldn't she? If she just weren't so tired. But she couldn't both sleep and see the stars, and she couldn't stand the days without the nights of stars.

The afternoon dragged through to the final bell. She hunched into a corner of her bus seat, willing herself not to look or listen to the other kids on the bus, yet unable to ignore the buzz and the stares.

At her stop, she hopped off and ran up the driveway, the sob that had choked her throat since lunchtime threatening to explode. She wouldn't cry. She wouldn't. They weren't worth crying about.

Grandma was sitting rocking in the kitchen. Angel wanted to run past her, go upstairs and throw herself down on her bed, but something in Grandma's face stopped her.

"What's the matter, Grandma?"

"I don't know. Something."

"What do you mean?"

"If I knowed, I could tell you, couldn't I? I just said I don't know."

Angel could feel her flesh crawl. She caught Grandma's fear. Something was happening, but she didn't know what it was. Dread was hanging over the house like dense fog on a mountain road.

"Where's Bernie?" she blurted out.

"At school." There was a pause. "I reckon."

Angel focused her mind on the elementary school. She willed herself to see Bernie there, straightening up his desk, saying goodbye to his teacher, walking out of the building, getting on the bus. In her heart she knew that wasn't the real Bernie, who would have resisted doing whatever every other kid did, but a different Bernie, a kind of robot Bernie, the kind that she could control in her imagination and make do the right things, the kind of Bernie she could make come home safe and happy.

"I guess I'll go wait for the bus." It was another forty-five minutes before it was due, but she needed to keep mental watch over the bus through its whole route, from the school door to Grandma's mailbox.

Grandma leaned back in the rocker and shut her eyes. She looked like something was paining her. That was it. The bad thing. Grandma felt sickly. She was an old lady. That was natural for old people, wasn't it? They had so many parts that didn't work so well anymore.

"Okay, Grandma?" she asked softly. "I'm just going out to the mailbox and wait for Bernie, okay?"

The old woman nodded without opening her eyes.

In light-years it was nothing, but in feeling time it was forever before she heard the shifting gears and saw the yellow bus coming over the brow of the hill. She waited, hardly breathing. If a doctor had put a stethoscope to her chest, he probably wouldn't even have detected a heartbeat. The bus rumbled past where she stood. It didn't slow, much less stop.

"Bernie!" she yelled at the back of it. She ran a few steps down the road behind it. "Bernie!" Unbelieving, she watched it bumping and rattling out of sight, heading for the corner, turning onto the paved road.

She raced back to the house.

Grandma sat up, eyes wide. "Where's Bernie?"

Angel was fumbling through the phone book. Why hadn't she kept the school number? *You always do that. Keep the number by the phone in case of emergency.* She was breathless now. The line was busy, of course. She slammed down the phone. *Oh Lord, I've forgotten the number.* Another fumble through the phone book. Another dial. At last that impatient voice of the secretary. "Chesterville Union Elementary School."

"Where's Bernie?" she blurted out, realizing too late that it was the wrong thing to say.

"Excuse me? Who did you want to speak to?"

She forced herself to be quiet a minute and took a deep breath. "This is Mrs. Verna Morgan. My son, Bernie, didn't get off the school bus just now—"

"Hold on a minute, please. I'll check."

"What she say? What she say?" Grandma was on her feet, wild-eyed, her head shaking.

"Shh. She's checking."

"Phht." Grandma made a funny sound with her lips.

"Who is this?" the secretary demanded.

Angel kept still.

"I'm asking because, according to the sign-out sheet, Mrs. Verna Morgan came by at twelve thirteen P.M. and picked Bernie Morgan up. It says here 'Doctor's appointment in Burlington.'"

Polaris

Grandma fell back into her rocker as though someone had smacked her in the face. "Doctor's appointment, my stuffed cabbage."

What was Verna doing? "Kidnapping! She kidnapped her own kid!" Angel was walking back and forth. She banged into a chair, sending it crashing to the floor, and didn't bother to pick it up. "She kidnapped Bernie! She didn't want me to know she was taking him. She didn't even come to get his clothes! I would have given him Grizzle. I would have." The tears were coming so hard now that she couldn't see where she was going, and she hit her hip against the edge of the table. She welcomed the pain. It gave her an excuse to cry all the more. What she didn't say—couldn't say out loud—was, *Why just Bernie? Why did she take Bernie and leave me behind? Doesn't she love me, too? Oh, Mama, I need you, too.*

"Sit down, Angel, before you break something past fixing."

She was suddenly ashamed. She went over and picked up the chair. "I'm sorry."

"I don't mean the danged chair. I mean you. Come here."

She went over to the rocker. Grandma had her skinny little arms out. "Here, in my lap, baby."

Even though she was almost bigger than the old woman, Angel sat down on the bony lap. The arms felt like sticks around her shoulders, but it didn't matter. She let go against them. She couldn't remember if she'd ever sat on anyone's lap and felt herself held and rocked.

"That Verna is a first-class bitch."

"No," Angel felt obliged to defend her mother. "That isn't it. She—she probably doesn't have enough money to take care of two kids, and Bernie's the baby. He needs her more than me."

Grandma snorted. Angel could feel the vibration of it through her ribs. "You're more of a mother to that boy than Verna ever was." It was like something Verna herself had said. But Verna must have forgotten who it was that really took care of Bernie.

Maybe she'd changed. Maybe now she would remember to make him eat all five food groups and wear his hat when it was cold outside and— Angel began to cry again, but softly this time.

"There, there," Grandma patted her. "I didn't mean to get you all roiled up. She'll probably bring him back by tomorrow. Ain't just anybody knows how to handle that little pricker bush."

Angel stood up. She needed a tissue badly, and

although she liked the thought of Grandma's lap, it was about as comfortable as cuddling with kindling. She went into the bathroom and got some toilet paper to blow her nose, not daring to look at herself in the streaky mirror. She knew she was a mess. "Grandma," she called from the doorway. "How about I make us some tea?"

"Well, that sounds downright civilized."

After the tea, even though it was still afternoon, Angel made supper for the two of them. They didn't talk much. They tried not to look at the place where Bernie should have been sitting. Grandma even ate her broccoli without complaining. Angel started to say something about it, but she could feel the tears start as she formed the sentence in her mind, and kept quiet. She washed the dishes and left them to dry beside the sink.

"I think I'll do my homework upstairs and then go on to bed," she said.

Grandma nodded from the rocker. Trying to be a comfort seemed to have worn her out.

Angel lay on her stomach under the bare bulb and opened *Know the Stars*. It was a page she'd read so often she could almost recite it.

Polaris (stress on LAR) is the only star that never changes its place in the sky, at least not so that you can notice it. It always stays put while the other stars and constellations are moving. . . .

That was what she needed—a Polaris, a North Star, that never moved. Something steady so that she could always find her way. But what about Bernie? She'd been his Polaris, hadn't she? When everything else had changed, at least he'd had her. Now he had Verna, who switched around faster than a whirling planet. She wished she knew how to pray. She wanted to pray for Bernie, for Verna, even for Wayne.

Wayne. He was her daddy. He never would have run off with Bernie and left her behind like Verna had. It wasn't his fault the police had thrown him in jail. He didn't even do it, whatever it was they said he did. He'd never even smacked her when she was little. He'd bought her Grizzle and given her her name, Angel. Did a man who named his baby girl Angel sound like somebody who would go off and commit a crime?

Even as she crept down the stairs, even as she took the phone off the hook, even when with her finger shaking she yanked around the dial the numbers she had memorized without ever meaning to, even until the moment the voice at the other end answered—something in her stomach warned her not to go ahead, her whispery voice as trembly as her body.

"This is Angel Morgan. I need to get a message to my daddy, Wayne Morgan. Just say . . . just say Verna's come and took Bernie off. Just tell him that."

She hung up the phone and went to the kitchen door to look out. She could smell frost in the air and hear the wind wailing in the changing leaves. It was a night of no stars.

★　★　★　★　★

Like a sleepwalker, she stumbled through the next day at school. She hadn't wanted to go at all. She'd wanted to stay by the phone, in case. But Grandma made her go. "It's like sitting in the garden watching cabbage come to a head. The phone'll never ring long as you're waiting beside it. Ask me. I know about such things."

She spent most of lunchtime in the bathroom and was still there in the stall when a group of girls swept in. "What did she say when you asked her about the robbery, Megan?"

Angel froze as Megan's voice answered the question. "Oh, she pretended she didn't know what I was talking about, but my grandma told my daddy and he told my mom that she's Wayne Morgan's girl. Grandma even had the clippings. She saves everything, and Daddy was in grade school with Wayne Morgan, so she thought he'd be interested."

Angel strained to hear the details. They might think she was pretending, but she really *didn't* know. It made her feel the fool to have Megan Armstrong know more about her daddy than she did.

"Did he shoot somebody?"

"He said he didn't, but the clerk had a bullet in him, didn't he? One of those guys in the ski masks shot him, and the other guys said Wayne Morgan did it. So it was two against one. They shouldn't ever let somebody like that out of jail."

But he didn't do it. Angel broke out in a cold sweat. *Wayne wouldn't hurt anybody.* But how did she know? She hardly knew her own daddy. It had happened when she was five, and all she could remember before that was the yelling. There must have been good times, too. Yes, when he bought her Grizzle. She remembered how happy she was when he gave her Grizzle. Verna had snorted something like "Blue bear? I swear," but Angel had loved it from the first. It was the only present he had ever given her, although for a while Verna would give her something and say "It's from your daddy and me." She had stopped saying it years ago. There hadn't been many presents, just the toys they got from the Salvation Army Santa Claus. That hardly counted.

The girls were still whispering, but whether about Wayne or something or somebody else, she didn't know. She wished they'd leave so she could come out of the stall. She read the dirty words and looked at the pictures scratched into the back of the door. You'd think the school would paint them over. Then again, some were dug deep in the door, so they'd probably show through the paint. She wished she had something with a sharp point, so she could scratch something nasty about Megan Armstrong on the door. Something that would last for years.

"Megan, shh! There's somebody in there."

"What of it?" Megan's voice answered. "Hey, you in there. You're not supposed to eavesdrop."

Angel stayed still, but she was seething inside. She'd been here when they came in, hadn't she?

"You scared to come out?" It was the voice of one of Megan's gang, Heather Somebody-or-other.

There was a giggle. "Hea-*thur!*"

Then suddenly Heather's head appeared under the stall door. The eyes went wide and quickly disappeared. "It's her in there!" she whispered fiercely.

"Everything I said was true. It was in the newspapers." Angel could almost see Megan tossing her bouncy curls.

"Let's get out of here," someone said. She could hear them scuffling out into the hall, whispering and giggling as they went. Angel was almost glad. For a few minutes she was able to think how much she hated those girls instead of the fact that Bernie was gone. *Gone.*

★ ★ ★ ★ ★

She slumped onto her bus seat with something like relief. The worst day of her life was coming to an end. Soon she'd be home. It was strange to think of Grandma's house as home, but it was. Home with a hole bigger than a moon crater, now that there was no Bernie in it.

"It didn't ring," Grandma said. She wasn't in her rocker. She was standing by the hot plate. "I'm fixing me some tea," she said. "You want some, too?"

Angel nodded. "Then I think I'll walk up to the library."

Grandma stiffened. "It's getting dark early," she said. "Tomorrow's Saddidy. Wait till tomorrow. Then you'll have time to shop, too. We must be out of one of them precious food groups by now."

Angel giggled despite herself. "You're catching on, Grandma. I'll have you trained yet."

They drank their tea in the darkening kitchen, their bodies in knots, fighting to keep from turning to stare at the phone. She'd always tried to defend Verna, always tried to see her mother's side of things, but it was hard to do this time.

★ ★ ★ ★ ★

She woke up in the night. She couldn't quite remember the dream that had awakened her. Someone—Bernie, she thought—had been crying, but the only fragment of the dream that had stayed with her was the sight of the pickup pulling away with Bernie's arm sticking out the window on the passenger side. "Pull in your arm, Bernie," she'd yelled. "How many times do I have to tell you? Get your arm out of the window!" She sat up, her throat as hoarse as though she'd been yelling out loud instead of in a dream.

She could still hear the crying. After countless nights of negotiating that black staircase, she was like a skillful blind person in the dark, making her way down to the kitchen and around the furniture until she reached the bedroom door. She leaned her head against the wood. Behind it she could hear the shuddering sobs of a broken old heart.

SIXTEEN

Consider the Heavens

There had been a hard frost in the night. The pasture was kissed with white, and beyond it the woods were a bonfire blaze of sugar maples. It might have seemed beautiful, if anything could look beautiful when her heart was so full of fearfulness and loss. When Angel reminded Grandma at breakfast that she was going to the library, the old lips trembled, and the old woman sniffed and blinked as if to hold back threatening tears.

"Is that okay?" Angel asked.

"Since when did you start needing permission from me?" The words were harsh, but Angel knew they weren't meant to be.

"I can go later."

Grandma threw out her hand. "No, no, go. Go on." Then she mumbled something Angel couldn't quite make out.

"What?"

"Nothing."

Grandma held some kind of grudge against Liza Irwin, that was plain, but Angel couldn't bring herself to ask what it was. She had enough problems of her own right now without digging into Grandma's unhappy past.

It was a cold morning. She wore her winter jacket. Had Bernie been wearing his when Verna picked him up? She hadn't dared check his things to see if it was missing. In August she'd not thought about mittens when she'd packed. Even though she was always nagging Bernie about wearing a hat, she never wore one herself. Today she almost wished for one. Her ears hurt from the cold, and it was barely fall—more than a month until Halloween.

Verna had taken them trick-or-treating last year. It had been fun—mostly. Bernie had gotten wild. He always did when he had too much sugar. Verna just laughed when Angel said that, and when Angel tried to make him save some of his candy for later, Verna called her a party pooper. So he ate way too much and began zooming around, screeching, acting like a crazy thing until Verna lost her temper and smacked him. Then he screamed and screamed and couldn't be shut up or calmed down for anything.

She mustn't think about things like that. Verna would've learned her lesson by now. She'd be a great mother, and Bernie himself was doing way better these days. Why, he'd be so happy to be with his mama again that he'd behave so well he'd never even meet the social worker at his new school. *You got to take him to school the first day, Mama. You got to see he gets settled in good. That'll get him off on the right track. It's important to start out right in a new place.* Even Grandma in her crazy way had given Bernie a good start here. *You wouldn't want Grandma to do better than you, now, would you, Mama?*

She lifted her eyes from the road and looked at the trees beside it. Could anything on earth be so beautiful as a sugar maple in the fall? She took a deep breath. The smell of frost was in the air. See? She wasn't going to stew about Bernie all day. She was going to trust that Verna had turned over a new leaf and was starting out as a first-class mother. But much as she tried, it was hard to pull her mind away from what had actually happened. Just like a kidnapping. Verna'd gone to the school and yanked him out and driven away, never even stopping at the house to get his things. *I would have given him Grizzle. He couldn't even say goodbye to Grandma, let alone me. She didn't want to hurt my feelings. That's why she did it that way. Because she was afraid that if she had to tell me that she could take only one kid, I'd cry or complain that she was leaving me and choosing Bernie. But I would've understood, really I would've. Bernie is the baby. I wouldn't have cried. I'd have said, "Sure, I understand." And she would have said that as soon as she was on her feet she'd come and get me, too. Wouldn't she have?*

She had to stop thinking. She was long past the broken house where they'd stopped for directions that first day and almost to the village. She had to get herself under control. She was swollen with tears trying to bust out, and she didn't want to be boo-hooing in front of Miss Liza, not to mention in the middle of the general store.

Well, she wouldn't be buying another box of those expensive Sugar Pops. That would help with the bill.

Funny, it was the thought of *not* buying Sugar Pops that burst the dam. She stood in the middle of the road and sobbed. Finally, she pulled a ratty tissue out of her pocket and blew her nose and wiped her eyes the best she could. Oh Lord, they were nearly out of tissues. She'd have to buy more. She concentrated on making a mental grocery list, so that by the time she got to the library, she was feeling if not better, then at least not on the verge of exploding into a Mississippi flood.

"Why, Angel, dear, what on earth is the matter?" Miss Liza asked the minute she saw Angel's puffy face. So Angel blurted it all out, how Verna had come and taken Bernie away. Soon they were sitting side by side on the low children's chairs in the picture-book section. Miss Liza had her head bent sidewise and her sharp little bird eyes on Angel's face, following every word of the long recital of events. "I'd just like to know where he's at and that he's okay," Angel said finally.

"Of course you would," Miss Liza said, handing her a fresh tissue. "So would I."

"But we can't call Welfare," Angel said quickly. "They won't know where they are, but if they think Verna is acting crazy, they'll hunt her down and take him away."

"Are you sure?"

"They did it before." Angel blew her nose. "She had a hard time getting us back." She needed to remember that—that Verna had fought like a wildcat to get them back. Bernie hadn't been much more than a baby the first time, and the last time Welfare had put them in two different foster homes. Home, ha! More like a reformatory. Angel had gotten whacked every time she'd turned around. She told the social worker, too. She heard one of the social workers say that Bernie had cried the whole two months they were separated. Maybe that's why Welfare gave them back to Verna in the end, because they'd made a mistake, putting her and Bernie into bad situations. She didn't tell Miss Liza all this.

"The other thing is . . ." Angel needed to word this carefully. "When Bernie doesn't show up at school on Monday, well, they may give it a few days, but then they're going to start calling and asking where he's at. Then what do I do?"

"That is a problem," Miss Liza said.

"Grandma—they won't talk to me, probably—Grandma can lie and tell them he's sick for just so long before they'll send someone out to investigate." She wished she hadn't said that about Grandma lying, but Miss Liza didn't remark on it.

"Are you thinking they might take you away, then?"

"It doesn't really matter about me."

"Yes, it does," Miss Liza said.

"I do need to stay on here for Grandma. You wouldn't believe what she eats when nobody's looking out for her. And she hardly gets out of her chair. She didn't get any exercise at all until she started walking Bernie to the bus stop and back. Now . . . well, if I'm not there to make her get out of that rocker . . . She really needs me."

Miss Liza smiled and patted Angel's knee with her crooked, brown-spotted hand, the veins standing up like blue ribbons under the papery skin.

"I've got an idea. It might not work . . ." *She's scared I'll get my hopes up.* "But I know the woman who is in charge of school libraries for the whole state. I'll ask her to find out if—that is, where—Bernie is enrolled. I'll tell her—oh, I'll tell her he failed to return a library book of mine. That's actually the truth."

"They go after kids for not returning library books?"

"Of course not. But I'll say, and I won't be lying—it's an absolute fact—that he's got a book that's hard to replace, so would they ask about it."

"Will that work?"

"Probably not. But I don't have a better idea." She sighed and patted Angel's hand again. They sat there, hearing no noise but their own breathing, until the wind blew a branch clattering against one of the windows. "How's the stargazing going?"

"Okay, I guess. I'm learning a lot from your book. It really helps."

"I miss it."

"I can bring it back."

"Oh, not the book. The sky."

Angel was confused. "The sky? How come?" The sky

wasn't like some overdue library book. It was always right there.

"My silly back," she said. "I can't turn my head up to see it properly."

"Oh."

"I can remember the stars. You mustn't feel bad for me."

"They're so huge, so far away. Sometimes," Angel said, "sometimes, when I think of them, I feel like I'm nothing at all."

"'When I consider thy heavens, the moon and the stars which thou hast ordained, what is man that thou art mindful of him?'" Miss Liza was quoting something. Angel waited until she paused. She figured Miss Liza would explain. "It's from the Bible," she said. "The eighth Psalm. I used to recite that to myself when I was studying astronomy. What is man—and of course the writer means all of us puny little insignificant creatures—what is a mere human being that God who made the immense universe should ever notice?" She chuckled. "The sky does take you down to size."

"Not even big as bugs. Not even a speck of dust to the nearest star," Angel agreed.

"But the psalmist answers his own question. 'Thou hast made him a little lower than the angels, and hast crowned him with glory and honor. . . .'"

"What?" Angel asked, not sure she had heard right.

"A little lower than the angels, crowned with glory and honor."

"The real angels? Do you believe that?"

"Yes, Angel, I do. When people look down on me, and these days"—she laughed shortly—"these days everyone over the age of five does. When people look down on me, I remember that God looks at this pitiful, twisted old thing that I have become and crowns me with glory."

Angel could hardly speak. There was pain in what Miss Liza said, terrible pain, but something else, too. Something Angel knew only when she turned her face to the stars. An awesome stillness. What was that word? A glory.

She left the library with three books and a heart too full to speak. In the grocery store she bought what she needed, wondering if the clerk and the three customers who were in and out noticed anything different about her. She felt so different from the girl who had left Grandma's house an hour or so before. Couldn't they see a little streak of shining in her, a bit of the glory Miss Liza had passed on to her?

Even when the clerk asked the very question she'd dreaded, "Where's your brother?" she looked her straight in her friendly, round face and said, "He's with my mom today." She didn't even have to lie.

★   ★   ★   ★   ★

"I brought you some ice cream, Grandma."

The old woman opened her eyes and roused herself up a bit from the chair. "It's probably cream soup by now," she grumped and closed her eyes again.

"No. She wrapped it special for you, so's it wouldn't get soft. Feel." She took the insulated bag over to the rocker.

Grandma touched it with one finger. "Hmmph."

"Want some now?"

"We ain't had our lunch yet."

"Dessert first, then lunch."

"What? I never heard such foolishness!" She let a ghost of a grin escape. "Where's Miss Five Major and Go Easy on the Sugar today?"

Angel giggled. "I sent her off on a little vacation. I figured you and me need a treat once in a while."

"Ohhhh-kay." Grandma pushed herself up out of the rocker. "Let me at it."

It was Rocky Road, with bits of marshmallow and nuts and streaks of dark chocolate through the milk chocolate.

"Hmmph," Grandma said. "Whoever heard of ice cream you have to chew? This is almost too much work for an old lady."

"You want me to finish yours for you?"

"Not on your stuffed cabbage."

They chewed and slurped the Rocky Road. "I guess there weren't any calls while I was gone." She knew there hadn't been, but still, just in case . . .

Grandma shook her head.

"I didn't think so." Did Bernie even know the number here? That was it—he didn't know the number. Otherwise, he would have called, wouldn't he? He wasn't tied up and gagged. He wasn't a prisoner. But he couldn't call because she'd never taught him Grandma's number. She should have taught him Grandma's number. They always tell you to teach little kids their address and phone number in case they get lost. She'd been too busy bossing him around to remember to teach him his own phone number. "I never taught him the phone number," she said aloud.

"Well, there, you see? How's he gonna call us if he don't know the number?"

They didn't eat much lunch—too filled up with Rocky Road. But it was just this once. She wouldn't do it again for a long time. Just once was okay, surely.

Angel got up to wash the dishes, trying to keep her mind off Bernie, trying to concentrate on what Miss Liza had told her, when Grandma's voice interrupted from the rocker: "You reckon I should buy a TV, Angel?"

"I don't know, Grandma. You want a TV?" *Can you afford a TV* was more like it. But she wasn't going to ask that.

"I used to have one, but it broke and I never missed it much. You can't get much up here in the country unless you pay for one of them dishes, and that costs more'n my grocery bill for a year."

"You don't need a TV."

"Well, I was thinking, maybe if I'd had a TV, Bernie would have stuck around. It's boring for a kid out here in the country, nobody to play with, nothing to do."

"I don't remember Bernie complaining about having no TV."

"Then you wasn't listening. He mentioned it to me nearly every day. I told him if I did have one, only thing he'd see was snow, and if he'd hold his horses for a couple of months, he'd see more snow than he'd ever want to." She shook her head. "I think he missed watching. I should have tried to get him one."

"Grandma, Bernie didn't leave because you didn't have a TV. He left because Mama came and took him. I bet he didn't even want to go."

"Yes, he did. He missed his mama. He told me that, too." She leaned back in her chair and closed her eyes. "I never was much of a mama, Angel."

"I bet you were, too. I bet you were a great mama."

"Jimmy and Ray, both my boys, spent time in jail. Now they're both dead. I don't know what I did wrong. I did the best I could."

"It's not your fault. Sometimes people are just unlucky. Or their children get in with the wrong crowd or something. You can't take the blame for that."

Grandma didn't seem to be listening. "I was on my own. My husband died when they was hardly more'n babies. I was trying to run this farm and raise two boys—I tried, Lord knows, but I guess I didn't have what it took. And then there was that damn war."

Angel kept scrubbing the same pot, trying to think of something to say, but no words came.

"Maybe they should have died over in Vietnam, but they didn't. They come home, both of them all messed up with drugs. Jimmy has to get married, but the baby's no sooner born than he's got himself in jail. Next thing I know, Ray's in jail as well. I couldn't understand that. Ray was smart. He was supposed to go to college." She closed her eyes and rocked, muttering something about the damn war before she continued. "So, my two boys are in jail, I got Jimmy's wife and baby living here—you want to talk about hell on earth—but it didn't last long. Just before she drives me stark raving crazy over the cliff, that no-count woman runs off with the cattle feed salesman and leaves Wayne behind. She didn't even change his diaper before she took off. Oh Lordy. I'd already failed with my own two boys. I guess I should have learned something, but"—she sighed deeply—"looks like I didn't. I s'pose it's a good thing Verna come and took Bernie off. I wouldn't want to ruin another generation of Morgans."

How could she comfort the old woman? Miss Liza had sat beside her and told her she was crowned with glory—but Angel wasn't Miss Liza. She didn't have the words to give Grandma. Finally, she said the only thing she could think to say.

"I'm still here, Grandma."

Grandma sat up a little and opened her eyes. "Yes, you are, ain't you?" She looked at Angel and nodded her head. "Can't be all bad if you got yourself an angel. Kinda bossy angel"—she glanced skyward—"but I guess I better not complain." She heaved herself out of the chair. "I'm going to bed. If the phone rings—"

"I'll get it. Don't worry."

SEVENTEEN

Galileo Galilei

Oh, this is a good night for viewing," the star man said, without even moving his eye from the telescope. "Come here." Angel went close enough to hear his breathing, which was raspy in the chill night air. He ought to dress more warmly and wear a hat. He ought, for heaven sakes, to stop smoking, but she might as well save her breath. He wouldn't listen.

"Now find Polaris."

It was easy for Angel to find the North Star now. Why had it seemed so hard last summer? You find the Big Dipper and let the two stars on its outer side point you straight to the North Star. There.

"Okay, look." His right arm swung upward beside her ear. "Up, up, almost straight up." She followed the sweep of his arm. "Can you see it? That little fuzzy patch up there? That's the Andromeda Galaxy. Want to see it in the telescope now?"

She nodded, too dazed to speak. She'd read about it in her book, but now she was actually seeing it. Andromeda! A whole other galaxy, a million—no, two million—light-years from earth, with a hundred billion stars swarming around inside it. She gasped at the beauty, the glory of the night.

And then the sharp pain of the days cut in. Bernie might as well be two million light-years away. "My brother's gone," she said.

"Oh?"

"My mom went and picked him up at his school and just took him away without telling me or Grandma."

He didn't say anything at first. Maybe he didn't care. She'd never mentioned Bernie to him before. He probably didn't even know Bernie existed.

"How's the old lady taking it?"

"Grandma?"

"Yeah."

"She's really upset. She and Bernie were good friends. They had a lot of fun together."

"He must have been good for her. Too bad he's gone." He took a pack of cigarettes out of his pocket and stuck one in his mouth. "I know I shouldn't," he said, as though to keep her from objecting, "but at least it's a legal addiction." He lit up and inhaled.

She watched the smoke coming from his mouth. Grownups had no sense. They didn't care what was good for them or bad for them. How did they ever get to be in charge of the world? "I got to go in," she said. "I haven't done my homework."

"I'm sorry about your brother," he said. "Your mom shouldn't have done that, should she?"

He didn't know how to say things the way Miss Liza did, but she could tell he wanted to help.

"No," Angel said, "she shouldn't have. Sometimes she doesn't figure things out right. She tries, but she just can't figure stuff out."

"I know how that is," he said. "I've done a lot of bad figuring myself." His voice sounded sad and tired. She wished she knew how to help him.

"It means a lot to me," she said, "you showing me the stars."

"It means a lot to me," he said, "you wanting to see them."

★   ★   ★   ★   ★

Every day when she got off the bus she hoped Verna's pickup would be parked by the house. Surely Verna would come back. She had never been able to manage Bernie on her own. She'd always left most of the responsibility to Angel. Bernie was, well, difficult to manage in the best of situations, and it was hard to imagine Verna in the best of situations. *She's changed. She's turned into a really good mother. She always loved Bernie. She always liked him better than me. Maybe I was the problem. Maybe without me butting in, she and Bernie are getting along just fine.* The thought was no comfort.

As the days went by and Bernie didn't come home, didn't call, her life took on a sort of pattern. In the morning she would get wood from the woodpile outside the kitchen door and make a fire in the big iron stove, bringing in enough extra wood so Grandma could keep warm all day while she was gone. Then she'd make breakfast for herself and Grandma, usually just cereal. At school, the whispers about Wayne had died down, and she was mostly ignored, which was fine with her. Just fine. She had learned to do her homework in the afternoon, in case it was clear that night. She didn't want homework hanging over her head. The days were getting short, so she usually had supper fixed by five o'clock, knowing that Grandma would go to bed soon afterward.

She hoped it would be warm at night, as the star man had told her not to come out if it was below freezing. "I'm having a little trouble getting over this cough," he said.

"You ought to wear a hat," she said, "and quit smoking."

He laughed. "Keep at it, Angel. You may reform me yet."

So when it was cloudy or freezing, she spent her evenings studying her star book and trying to memorize the names of all the bright stars and the constellations. In the section on autumn stars there were two north views of the sky and two south views. On the left, there was a picture that looked like the actual sky looking north or south. On the right, the constellations were connected like those connect-the-dots books. It helped a lot to have the connect-the-dots pictures. You had to admit that the real sky looked like God or whoever had picked up a bucketful of different-sized jewels and just flung them out against the dark.

Of course, the stars didn't know their names. They didn't even know they belonged together in a picture of a bear or a horse or a woman chained to a rock, waiting for a whale to swallow her up. That was all in people's imaginations. People had turned the stars into pictures and stories to make them seem more manageable. Otherwise, all the immenseness would just sweep a person away like a giant wave. *What is man?* Even when people hadn't known about galaxies millions of light-years away, hadn't even known about light-years, the stars had been awesome.

When they had library period at school, the reading teacher usually took her to shelves with the easy books. She wasn't sure why. She could read well enough, but one morning just before Halloween they had a sub, who let Mrs. Coates, the librarian, take charge. There was no way Angel was going to choose those silly little stories for herself, but she didn't know how to find what she wanted, so for a minute she just stood in the middle of the floor.

"Can I help you find something, Angel?" It was Mrs. Coates. "What kind of book are you interested in?"

"I—I like books about stars," Angel blurted out.

"Oh. Then I have the perfect book for you," Mrs. Coates said and started over to the picture-book section. Angel hesitated. At least Ms. Bridgeman, the language-arts teacher, didn't try to make her read picture books.

Mrs. Coates bent over, picked a book off the shelf, and stood up. Angel had yet to move, so Mrs. Coates called over to her, "Angel, trust me, you're going to love this book."

The title of the book was *Starry Messenger,* and it was written and illustrated by someone named Peter Sís. Ever since she'd fallen in love with H. A. Rey, she had paid more attention to authors. On the cover of Mr. Sís's book was a man looking through what had to be an old-timey telescope. He was on the porch or balcony of a tower. Painted on the tower were animals, which she soon realized represented the constellations. She opened the book to see a star-splattered night over a deep-blue cityscape. Only one light shone in the sleeping city. It was a window in a tower. In the window was the man with his telescope pointed at the sky.

"Beautiful, isn't it?"

"Yes." Angel breathed the word. "Can I take it out?"

"Of course."

Angel didn't go to the checkout desk. She plunked herself down in the nearest chair, never closing the book.

The man in the tower was named Galileo Galilei. It was as if she'd been named Morgana Morgan or Angel Angelina. It was a little bit silly, but the man himself was not silly at all. He was a "famous scientist, mathematician, astronomer, philosopher, physicist." *Whew.* A man who knew everything but who thought he had to prove *how* he knew it to other people, and he did it by making the first telescope to be aimed at the stars. He wanted to prove that the sun was the center of the universe—not the earth, as most people believed.

This made the authorities so angry that they put him on trial and then locked him up in his house with someone guarding him. It was exactly like putting him in jail for the rest of his life. Finally, they had to admit he was right, but Galileo Galilei had been dead for 350 years when they said so. They gave him a pardon. That was the crazy part. They forgave *him* for their own mistake. It didn't make sense.

Yes, it did, in a funny kind of way. Wasn't she always wanting Verna to forgive *her*? Didn't Verna have some apologizing to do herself? Not to mention Wayne. Why should she feel like apologizing to Wayne, especially if he really had robbed that convenience store and shot that clerk like they said? *Maybe kids cost so much money* . . . No. It was not her fault that Wayne had robbed that store. She hadn't asked for anything. If Verna had tried to make him feel he had to have more money, well, that was Verna's fault, not hers. Wasn't it?

"Angel! Stop daydreaming! It's time to go back to class." Megan Armstrong was standing over her, trying to see what book she was lost in. Angel tried to put her arm over the book to hide it. "It's a *picture* book! You're not checking out a *picture* book, are you?" She made sure all her friends could hear her.

"I've already checked it out for you, Angel," Mrs.

Coates called from the desk. "If you need any other books on astronomy, just let me know, all right?"

"Astronomy?" Angel could tell Megan was impressed.

"Thank you, Mrs. Coates," Angel said, ignoring Megan's open mouth. "If you have another one on Galileo Galilei, would you save it for me?" She moved past Megan into the line that was forming at the door. She could hear Megan and the others buzzing behind her, but this time she wasn't embarrassed. She knew they were trying to figure out how someone like Angel knew about astronomy and Galileo Galilei.

The star man would love this book, but how could she show it to him in the dark? Even if she borrowed Grandma's huge flashlight, the beam was hardly enough to make out the details in the pictures, much less read the print and the funny way the artist had written other stuff around the pages in script. *Starry Messenger* was gorgeous, almost as wonderful as the sky itself. It made H. A. Rey's *Know the Stars* look poor and homely. Still, the two books had one thing in common: she never wanted to have to return either of them to the library.

She hid the book inside her notebook and read it the rest of the day. By the time she got off the bus, she had read the story at least twice and had read nearly everything that was written in script in the illustrations as well. It was almost as exciting as seeing Andromeda. She wondered if Galileo had been able to see that through his homemade telescope.

Out of habit, she checked the mailbox. It was empty except for a flyer urging Occupant to go to a sale at the Wal-Mart in Berlin. Fat chance! She balled up the flyer in her hand. She wondered if they'd had advertisements in Galileo's time. She knew they had had a printing press, because Galileo's own book had been published. But they sure as heck didn't have Wal-Mart flyers! She giggled.

She caught herself dancing up the driveway and made herself slow down. If she was too happy when she walked through the door, Grandma was likely to ask how come. Then she'd either have to lie, which got complicated, or show her the book, which would take an explanation, an explanation that would have to include not only Miss Liza but the star man. She'd never mentioned the star man to Grandma. And the longer she waited the harder it got. What would Grandma say if Angel told her about him. If Grandma thought at all, she would probably wonder what a little girl was doing out with a grown man after dark. "Looking at the stars." Even though that was the honest and total truth, it didn't sound believable somehow.

Grandma was sitting in her chair in the near dark. Angel flipped on the switch by the door. "I'm back, Grandma."

Grandma blinked in response to the sudden light. "Well, I ain't blind or deaf yet. And no, the drat phone ain't rang all day."

She'd better tone down her mood to match Grandma's.

"Can I make you some tea, Grandma?"

"I hate tea."

"No, you—" Angel stopped midprotest. "Okay."

"I'm bored," Grandma said. "Ain't nothing to do around here."

"Well, I could read to you."

"You already read them books. Ain't you got nothing new to read?"

"I could run down to the library."

"No!" Grandma sat up straight. "You'd just go off blabbing about all our troubles to Liza Irwin. I don't like that smarty-pants butting her nose into my family business. You ought to know that by now, girly!" She slumped against the back of the rocker. "Didn't you bring something new home from school?"

How could she know? "I don't think you'd like it."

Grandma closed her eyes. "I guess I could be the judge of that," she said.

She slung her backpack off her shoulder and onto the table and took out *Starry Messenger.* Grandma had her eyes shut and was gently rocking back and forth, so maybe Angel could just skip the pictures and the script— just read the words in print. "For hundreds of years, most people thought the earth was the center of the universe, and the sun and the moon and all the planets revolved around it. . . ."

"That ain't true. People don't think no such thing."

"No, Grandma, that's what the book—"

"I'm telling you, people don't give a flip about the rest of the world, much less the blinking universe. They just care about themselves. I been sitting here all these days trying to figure out that mother of yours. That's exactly her problem. She thinks she's the center of the universe, and you and me and Bernie and even poor old Wayne is just something to whirl around her every want and wish. Well, I tell you, she is wrong, one hundred and forty percent wrong."

"Yes, Grandma." While the old woman ranted on, Angel slipped the precious book back into her pack and set about making tea.

★　★　★　★　★

It was a wonderfully warm night for late October, and the sky was as bejeweled as the pictures inside the cover of *Starry Messenger.* She decided to take the book outside and try to show the star man the pictures by Grandma's flashlight. He'd probably want to take it home to look at better, but she'd just explain that it was a school library book and you weren't allowed to lend it to anybody else. He'd understand that. Even if he didn't seem to worry about rules, she was sure he'd think that the school had plenty of them for kids to follow.

When there were no more sounds from the kitchen, Angel went downstairs. She was wearing her winter jacket. It wasn't really cold, but by ten or so she'd be glad she had it. She got the big flashlight from the drawer in the cabinet nearest the door and tiptoed out, pulling the door gently behind her. Tonight of all nights she didn't want Grandma hearing her sneak out.

He wasn't there. It was a perfect night, balmy as summertime, and he wasn't there. All that worry about if or how to share her library book and he wasn't even out there where he was supposed to be, where he always was when the night was clear and warm. She went on out to the field, looking right and left, sweeping the flashlight in great swaths across weedy land. He was nowhere to be seen. She headed toward the trailer. Maybe he was just late tonight. But when she got closer, she could see that there were no lights on in the trailer, and his old car was missing.

Why had he gone away? Was it because he somehow knew she didn't want to share *Starry Messenger* with him? No, that didn't make good sense. She must have done something to hurt his feelings or make him not want to be with her anymore. That was it. She racked her brain for what she might have said the last time they were together. She'd nagged him about his smoking. No. That wasn't it. Face it. It was because she was too dumb. She couldn't see all the things he wanted her to see and so he'd lost patience with her. He didn't want to be bothered with someone so slow that it took her a couple of weeks to be sure where Polaris was—the one star that hardly moved, and—

No! She wiped away a tear with the back of her hand. She was not stupid. She had to stop telling herself stuff like that. It was *him*. *He* was letting her down. Just like

everyone else. That's what grownups did. They got kids
to trust them, and then they just let go—*blam*. They
didn't know what it felt like to be dropped like that, or
they didn't care. To the kid being dropped, it hurt just the
same whether the grownup was being mean or careless.
It felt the same to the kid. And it wasn't the kid's fault,
either! It wasn't. The first time a social worker had told
her that, it had just melted on her ears like snow. But now
she knew it was true. At least in her head she knew it was
a fact. All the things that had happened to her and Bernie
hadn't been their fault. She was sick and tired of thinking
it was her fault when they got left at cold apartments and
all-night diners and grandmas and, and— She turned
and, stumbling over the uneven ground, ran back toward
the safety of the house, clutching Galileo Galilei under
one arm and trying to follow the bouncing light of the
flashlight through a mist of tears.

She was never going to trust anyone again. Not even
Mrs. Coates. Not even Miss Liza. Not even— She could
hardly breathe. Her toe caught on the doorsill, and she
fell, the flashlight bouncing and rolling, rattling across
the kitchen floor until it came to a noisy stop against a
chair leg.

"What's that!" Grandma's voice cried out from the
bedroom.

"Just me," Angel said.

"My gawd, girl! You trying to scare the liver out of
me?"

"I'm sorry. I tripped." Angel got up. She felt bruised all over. Even her heart felt sore. "Just go back to sleep, Grandma. It's okay." She closed the door as quietly as she could and slid the flashlight into the drawer. When she turned around, Grandma was standing in the doorway.

"Turn on the light, girl. No wonder you nearly broke your neck. Wandering about the kitchen in the dark. I thought you had some brains in that head."

"I'm sorry, Grandma."

"Just turn on the light, silly."

Angel switched on the light by the door.

"You thinking of running out on me?"

"No."

"Then why are you standing by the kitchen door wearing your winter coat?"

"Oh, that."

"Yeah, that." Grandma's gray hair was out of its day-time bun and was streaming down her shoulders, making her look like a witch in a bad movie.

"I—I couldn't sleep. I just thought—"

"You lying to me?"

"Why should I lie to you?" Angel could hear the lie in her own voice, but maybe Grandma would be fooled.

"I don't know," said Grandma, shaking her head. "It happens." She went toward the rocker, moving as though she were a hundred years old instead of eighty. She eased herself down and then looked up at Angel, still standing by the door, the lie pasted all over her face.

"Make us some tea, won't you, angel girl?"

"Sure."

"And take off that dratted jacket. It scares me." Her voice was almost a whimper.

They sat there, drinking the scalding tea, not speaking, Angel sinking into shame. It was just like the times she had let Bernie down, making him scared that she, too, would desert him, when she never would have. He had to know that. Even now. He wouldn't think that she had *wanted* to be left behind, would he? Had Verna told him that Angel was tired of looking after him and that was why . . .

The tiredness of the last few days had seeped into her bones. She felt almost too heavy to climb the stairs and go to bed, but what else was there to do? Wayne left, then Verna, then Bernie, and now the star man—all gone without a word.

"I'm going to bed now, Grandma," she said.

"Yeah," the old woman said, but she didn't make a move out of her chair.

EIGHTEEN

Falling Stars

The next afternoon when she got off the bus, she felt the man's presence before she saw him. He seemed taller than he did in jail, as he stepped out of the trees beside the road.

"Angel?"

"Daddy?" She squinted her eyes at him, hardly believing what she saw. He was supposed to be in jail, not here. "What are you doing here?"

"I'm sort of like on parole," he said, blinking his eyes and cocking his head like Bernie did when he was set to defy her. "You sounded upset on the telephone, so I thought I better come."

"Parole?"

"Yeah." He gave a smirk. "For good behavior." She stood unmoving in the road, not knowing what to say or think. Was he lying to her?

"Ain't you going to give your daddy a hug?" he asked, coming toward her. She wanted to run, but how could she run from him, her own daddy? She put her arms loosely around his shirt, which smelled like sweat and tobacco. He seemed not to notice how quickly she stepped back. "I'll tell Grandma you're here," she said, turning away from him.

"I don't think that's a good idea, sweetheart. She don't like me much. I got a friend going to pick me up later. Maybe I'll just stay in the trailer till he gets here."

"You can't do that." Her voice was sharper than she'd meant it to be. "Someone else lives there now."

"Oh," he said. "Well, I guess it'll have to be the sugar shack, then. You could bring me out something to eat, couldn't you?" He gave a short laugh. "I'm like to starve."

So he had run away and was expecting her to hide him. She wanted to tell him to go away, to go back to wherever he was supposed to be, before the cops came pounding on the door again, before what little was left of her world got broken into a million pieces. Instead, she walked beside him up the driveway, with his left hand on her right shoulder. She was sure the weight of it would leave a mark, like a handprint, right through her jacket and sweatshirt and onto her skin. "Sooner the better. I'm ready to eat a horse." He squeezed her shoulder before he let go and headed for the sugar shack.

She watched him disappear inside, her heart pounding. What was she to do with him? If she told Grandma, Grandma was sure to call the police. Wayne was right. The old lady didn't like him—was scared of him, more than likely. She herself should probably call the police, but you can't call the police to take away your own daddy. If only the star man were here. She glanced across to the trailer, but there was no car there. Miss Liza had said to call whenever she needed help, but this wasn't the kind of burden to lay on the crooked shoulders of an old lady. She went into the house. She needed time to think.

"You're late."

"Am I?"

"What you been up to?" The eyes from the figure in the rocker were narrowed in suspicion.

"Nothing. I just got off the bus. It must have been late today."

The old woman stuck out her lip in a pout. "I ain't had no lunch."

"Grandma! I left you a sandwich in the fridge. I told you it was there."

"I didn't feel like peanut butter."

"Well, what do you feel like?"

"I don't know. I don't have no appetite lately."

Angel wanted to scream. How could she figure out what to do about Wayne in the sugar house while Grandma was in here acting for all the world like a spoiled seven-year-old? She opened the refrigerator door. There wasn't much inside. A little milk, one egg, the heel ends of a loaf of bread, a half jar of grape jelly, a dish of leftover peaches. No ham, no meat of any kind. Men always expected meat, didn't they? "I guess I better hightail it to the store before it closes," she said.

"No!"

The sharpness of the command made Angel turn quickly.

"It—it gets dark too soon. I don't want you to leave me here in the dark by myself."

"It's okay, Grandma, I can get off the bus at the store tomorrow and bring stuff home then." She went to the cabinet. There were always beans in the cabinet. She didn't think she'd ever bought any. Sometimes it seemed like the beans got together and multiplied on the shelf. "I'll just heat up a can of beans, okay?"

"Hmmph."

She took the grunt for a yes. As she stirred, her mind went back to Wayne. It would be cold out there in the sugar house. Should she try to sneak him a blanket? She could take him the peanut butter sandwich Grandma hadn't eaten, but there wasn't much else. Well, it wasn't her fault he came without any notice. She tried to ignore the churning in her stomach.

"Why don't you come over to the table to eat your beans, Grandma?" She had the feeling the old woman hadn't moved all day. At first she thought Grandma was going to refuse, but she grunted her way out of the rocker and across the short distance to the kitchen table.

The only sound at the meal was the noise Grandma made with her lips as she ate. Finally, she said, "You scared me, Angel." The long white hair growing out of the mole on her nose was trembling as she spoke.

"How did I scare you?"

"I thought you was running out on me for sure."

"Why would you think that?"

"Well, you was out last night late and then you was late coming home."

"I haven't got anyplace to run to, Grandma."

"Some folks don't need no place. They just go."

Like Wayne. Like Verna and Bernie. Like the star man.

"Well, I got better sense than that. 'Sides, I just about got you trained to the five major food groups. I wouldn't want to have to start all over with somebody new."

Grandma gave a tiny hint of a grin.

★   ★   ★   ★   ★

Angel did her homework at the kitchen table, all the time trying to figure out how to get the sandwich and a blanket out to Wayne, trying not to hate him for mixing up her life worse than it already was. She thought Grandma would never go to bed, and even after she had, it was a long time before Angel could hear the snores that proved the old woman was dead asleep.

She took the quilt off the bed in the room that should have been Verna's. She couldn't bring herself to take Bernie's, even though it was a single. In the kitchen she got a Mason jar and filled it with water, grabbed the wax-paper-wrapped sandwich, and crept out to the sugar shack.

She pushed open the door. "Daddy?"

"I thought you wasn't ever coming." She couldn't see his face, just the shape of him sitting on the floor, leaning against the case of encyclopedias.

"I had to wait until Grandma was asleep. I didn't think you wanted me to tell her you were here."

"No. No. I'm sorry. I'm just starving to death. What you got?"

"Just a peanut butter sandwich and some water. But I brought you a blanket. And tomorrow I'll go to the store and get something better."

"No need for that. We're going to be out of here before morning."

The leftover sweet smell of years of boiled sap stung her nose, mixed with the smell of mold and sweat and— The words burst out: "Have you been smoking?"

"Just a couple cigarettes. It's cold as hell in here."

"What if you start a fire?"

"Verna warned me you was a little Miss Worrywart." He gave a sort of chuckle. "I'll be careful, promise."

"And smoking can kill you."

"You do care about your old daddy, don't you?" He patted the floor beside him. "Here. Keep me company while I eat."

She sat down beside him, not knowing quite what to say. She wanted to ask why he was here and was he really on parole, but the words stuck in her throat.

"Remember that time we went to the fair and I won that bear for you?"

"I still got him," she said.

"You're kidding! You still got that damn bear?"

"Yeah."

He put his right arm, the one holding his sandwich, around her shoulder so that some of the peanut butter smeared on her jacket sleeve. "I can't hardly believe that. You kept that bear all these years? I never." He pulled her close and took a bite of the sandwich in front of her face. She liked the feel of his strong arm around her shoulder. The only sound for a long while was his chewing the sandwich, Grandma's sandwich.

"I gotta go back in, Daddy," she said, getting up from the floor.

"Hold it a minute. I got to tell you something. Real good news."

She stood by the door, waiting.

"I'm not ever leaving you again. Ain't that great?"

"I don't understand. You said . . ."

"I'm taking you with me. That's the reason I come back. To get my angel girl."

She began to tremble so hard that she leaned against the door and grabbed the knob.

"Angel?"

"What, Daddy?"

"Ain't that great news?"

"Yes, Daddy." Why didn't it feel like good news?

"Now, you go to the house and pack whatever little things you need to take along and then come right back. My buddy promised he'd be here round midnight, and best I can make out"—he was holding his wrist up, try-ing to see his watch—"it's past eleven already."

Her teeth were chattering, and her legs wobbled so much she could hardly make it to the kitchen door. She stole into the house and up the stairs. Yanking the green suitcase out from under the bed, she threw it on top of the quilt. There was no way her hands could work well enough to fold her clothes. She just grabbed them out of the drawer, stuffed them in the bag, and shakily pulled the zipper. Then she crept back downstairs, closing the kitchen door behind her as quietly as she could. Everything about her was shaking except her mind, which felt like her mouth had that time the dentist at the clinic punched it with a huge shot of Novocain.

He was standing just inside the sugar shack door when she opened it. "You came," he said, drawing her in and closing the door behind her. "I was afraid you wouldn't."

She nodded in the darkness. This is what she'd wished for, wasn't it? That he'd never leave her again?

He sat down against the encyclopedia shelves. "We'll show old Verna, won't we?" he said.

What did Verna have to do with it? "I don't understand."

"She took my boy, but she ain't getting my angel girl."

What did he mean? That she was only something to be kept from Verna, like some piece of property he didn't want stolen?

"Yeah, soon as they let me out this morning, I knowed it was my one and only chance. I'm going to take you so far away she'll never see you again. How about Florida? Would Florida suit you, baby?"

Florida? What was he talking about? Even if he really was on parole, he couldn't go running around wherever he pleased. Angel knew enough about the system to know that. "They won't let you go to Florida without permission, will they?"

"Hell, they won't even let you go to the bathroom without permission, but you don't have to worry about that, baby. Your daddy is doing the worrying from here on out."

"Daddy?"

"Yeah, angel girl?"

"I forgot my bear. I need to go back and get my bear."

"You got a thing about that bear I give you, don't ya? Sure, go get your bear, baby, just hurry, okay? He'll be here before long." She started for the door. "And Angel, if the old witch has any cash, better bring that, too."

"All she's got is her Social Security, Daddy. You can't take that."

"Hell, she owes me a lot more than that for all the crap I took off her."

Angel couldn't move. He wanted her to steal from Grandma.

"Go on, baby, we ain't got much time."

She left, pulling the door shut behind her, but instead of going into the kitchen door, she turned, making a wide circle toward the back fence, and then ran like the devil was at her heels to the trailer. The star man's car was still missing, but maybe—yes, the door wasn't locked. People didn't seem to bother locking doors out here in the country, though they ought to—you didn't know who might turn up. She flopped down on a couch under the window and sat there panting until she got her breath under control. Then she waited.

Finally, she heard the sound of a car coughing up the dirt road and saw the lights as they swept left into Grandma's driveway. Wayne came out of the sugar shack. She couldn't hear what he was saying to the driver, but by the moon's light she could see him beside the driver-side window, his head bobbing up and down in agitation and then swiveling toward the house as if looking for someone. At one point he picked up some gravel out of the driveway and flung it at one of the upstairs windows. *That's the wrong window, Daddy. That's Verna's room.* At last he walked around and got into the passenger seat and slammed the door and the car drove off. He never even looked in the direction of the trailer. As the car backed down to the road, she could just make out the shape of her suitcase standing by itself in the middle of the driveway, where Wayne had left it.

When the sound of the motor died away, she sat, like somebody frozen. He had come to get her, and she'd run away from him. Little Miss Obey All the Rules. That's what happened to people who always obeyed. Life went whizzing by, and they just sat there cold and lonely like the ice in the South Pole. She didn't have any tears. A real daughter would have cried for her daddy, who was leaving her and running away to Florida and probably ruining his life.

It was almost morning before she made herself get up from the couch to go to her own bed. The star man's things were all around her—his books, his telescope, even the smell of him. Where had he run to? She would have gone with him if he had asked her to. No, how could she have thought that she could leave Grandma? Someone had to be her Polaris.

★ ★ ★ ★ ★

She crept back into the house, but she couldn't sleep. Her brain was like a little car on a giant amusement park ride, going up and down and round and round, upside down and flinging her from one side to the other, making her want to vomit. She would have screeched out loud if she hadn't been afraid that Grandma would hear.

The next day she got through school, grateful that the numbness was back in charge of her brain. She spoke to no one at school. She didn't even stop to see Miss Liza when she went to the store. She hardly spoke to Grandma that evening. They ate a silent supper, and when the phone shrilled, they both jumped in their seats. They sat transfixed, listening to the phone scream, watching it vibrating on the wall.

"Well," Grandma said after the seventh ring, "you'd better get it. It might be Bernie."

Angel forced herself up from the chair, walked to the phone, and lifted the receiver, not daring to hope it was Bernie, and praying it wasn't the police or social services. It was a stranger, asking for Mrs. Morgan. Female strangers meant social services.

"They want you." Angel turned to Grandma, breathing hard.

"If they're selling, I ain't buying."

"Mrs. Morgan can't come to the phone right now," Angel said in her Verna voice. "Can I take a message?"

"This is the Central Vermont Hospital," the voice said. *Oh, God, not Bernie.* "We have a Ray Morgan here as a patient. He wanted Mrs. Morgan to be informed of his impending operation."

"Who'd you say was having an operation?"

"What'd she say?" Grandma was on her feet. "Lemme talk." She came and took the phone out of Angel's hand. "This is Miz Morgan," she said. "What's going on?"

There was nothing for Angel to do but wait. At first, she could only feel relief that the call was neither about Bernie nor the police asking after Wayne. It wasn't even Welfare on her tail. It took several minutes before dread like icy fingers began to claw at her. Who was in the hospital? Ray Morgan was dead. Grandma had said so.

Grandma wasn't saying much, mostly nodding, as though to show the caller she understood. She was obviously getting a lengthy explanation, at the end of which, she said, "How 'bout doing that once more in English?"

Another explanation. "Oh. Oh. Yeah. Okay. No, I guess not. Okay. Yeah." After which she hung up. When she turned away from the phone, her eyes were wide, like an animal caught in the headlights of an onrushing car.

"He's gonna die," she said. "I just know it."

"Who? Who's going to die?" Angel could hardly breathe.

Grandma made her way back to the rocker like a person in great pain. "Santy Claus," she said and began to rock, her eyes and face still paralyzed.

NINETEEN

Stardust to Stardust

Grandma, there's no such thing as Santa Claus." She could feel a chill spreading to her stomach as she said it.

The old woman looked up at her with eyes as sad as a little child's. "Well, I guess you ought to know."

"Still, someone has been helping you out all these years. Was that Ray—your son Ray?" *The star man?*

"I ain't got no sons nor grandsons nor great-grandsons neither."

"The woman from the hospital said Ray Morgan."

"And just what does she know about anything?"

"The man who's in the hospital told her he was your son Ray. She was just passing his message along."

"My Ray died a long time ago. He went to the army and died in that there Vietnam. He never come back to me." She closed her eyes and began to rock. "The government took away my baby boy, and he never come back."

She didn't want to ask, didn't even want to know, but she had to. "Then who—who's living in your trailer?"

"What do you know about somebody living in the trailer?"

"Me and Bernie were looking around the property, and we peeked in the window. Somebody lives in there."

"You got no right to go poking your nose in places that ain't none of your beeswax."

"I know. But I did it anyhow."

"You ain't seen nobody around, have you?"

"Well, the first night we were here, Bernie thought he saw a man down in the yard with a gun."

"*You* ain't seen nobody then?"

She wanted to lie. She didn't want the star man to be Grandma's strange, not quite alive, son.

"I asked you, Did you see anybody around?"

"Well, somebody kept bringing us groceries. And I knew it couldn't be Santa Claus like you said."

"I'm a crazy old woman, Angel."

"No, you're not! And I'm not going to let you use that for an excuse. You don't want me lying to you. Well, I'm sick and tired of you lying to me." Her voice was high pitched and much louder than she meant for it to be.

"You tell me something first." The old woman leaned forward, suddenly cagey.

"What?" asked Angel.

"You tell me how come you're all interested in stars?"

There was no use lying, but she didn't know how to begin on the truth. So she just stood there, trying to think.

"You seen Ray. I know. There is two people around here who is star-crazy. One is Liza Irwin and the other is

Ray Morgan. I know you seen Liza, but I'm thinking you been sneaking out at night to see Ray."

"How could I see Ray? Ray is dead. You said so yourself."

"I said *my* Ray was dead. They killed him over there, and the thing that come back was this—this zombie. You know what a zombie is?"

"Like a ghost?"

"Exactly. He wouldn't talk. He couldn't work. He just spooked the hell out of me. He weren't my little boy. I kept throwing him out of the house. He'd come back, promising to get off the drugs. Next thing I knew he was stealing my TV or my Social Security check. I throwed him out again."

"But you let him live in the trailer."

"That was later. After he was in jail. He come out, he's sick, and he don't have no place to go. I ain't letting him in *my* house again. Not on your stuffed cabbage. He's not my boy. He's some stranger wearing my boy's face for a Halloween mask. He's over there in the trailer, he ain't on the streets, but I don't have to see him. I don't have to pretend he's somebody I use to care about."

She wiped her face on her dress skirt, glancing up to see Angel staring down at her. "I'm not crying over Ray. I finished crying over him years ago. I'm crying over all the waste of lives this house has seen. I been here all this time, watching the waste of manhood, but I can't make it stop. I lost my boys, so I thought when that tramp left

Wayne to me, I could do it right this time. Well, nobody knows better'n you how I failed there, Lord save us." She tore at the side of her dress like she wanted to rip it. "Then I thought maybe with Bernie— You was so good with the boy. I thought maybe you and me together could put a stop to all these generations of losers, but your mama took care of that, didn't she?" She sighed deeply. "I just pray to God I don't live long enough to see that boy go to jail. That's all I ask. To die before that happens. I can't stand no more failure, Angel. I just can't."

"You didn't fail with Ray, Grandma."

"The hell I didn't."

"No, you didn't. You're right. I *have* seen him. I've seen him lots of times. On clear nights I go out, and he teaches me about the stars. At first I was so dumb, I couldn't see anything, but he's so patient, he just tells me over and over. His heart is almost big as the sky, Grandma. Anybody would be proud to have him for a son. Really."

Grandma lifted her face from her apron and stared at Angel as though she was trying to suck the light out of Angel's eyes. "You ain't lying to me. You think he's a good man, don't you?"

"I know he is, Grandma. I ought to know. Where I've had to live there are plenty of bad ones. He's a really good man, and he wants to see you." Angel went over to the old woman's chair and knelt beside her. "Children need their mamas, Grandma. Doesn't matter how old they are."

"Hmmph."

Angel stood up. "Well, I'm going to call Miss Liza in the morning and see if she can find somebody to give me a ride to the hospital. I'm going to visit him even if you won't."

"You and your danged Miss Liza! She was always so smart and good. Everybody loved Liza Irwin, even when we was kids. Then Ray—who did he go running to ever time he was hurting? Not to me, his own mama. No. It was his precious Miss Liza, who comes telling me I got to let him live in the trailer. Well, I let him, didn't I?"

"Grandma, it's okay. Really. He called you. He wants to see you. I know he loves you."

"Go to bed. You got no business being up so late."

"Okay. But you think about what I said, all right?"

In reply, Grandma just sniffed.

Angel went on to bed. She lay there reviewing the last crazy days. The star man missing. Wayne showing up. Her almost going missing, too. The star man . . . No, she wouldn't think of him dying. He was just going to have an operation. Nor would she think of Wayne being tracked down and heading back to jail.

★ ★ ★ ★ ★

Miss Liza called her great-nephew Eric, and the two of them appeared at about eleven the next morning. Angel had been ready since she called the librarian at nine. Grandma was still in her bathrobe.

"You coming, Grandma?" Angel asked when she heard the car drive up.

"I don't like Liza Irwin. Never have."

"This doesn't have anything to do with you and Miss Liza. This is about you and Ray."

"I don't feel so good."

There was no use begging or arguing. Angel grabbed her jacket and went out to where the old Buick waited. Miss Liza, her head almost on her lap, was in the passenger seat, so Angel got in the back. Miss Liza twisted her head to speak to her. "Is Erma coming?"

"She says she doesn't feel well."

"Oh."

The ride into Barre was mostly a silent one. Occasionally, Miss Liza's great-nephew—he looked to be about twenty-five, though Angel had no real way of judging the age of a grownup—said something quietly to Miss Liza, who answered in a few also quiet words. She was thinking, Angel could tell, but what she was thinking Angel had no way of knowing.

She stared out the window at the bleak late-autumn landscape. . . . Today was Halloween. It fit somehow with all the craziness of her life—all the ghosts, all the goblins. The trees had long since dropped their leaves, which lay brown and soggy in the ditches and across the road. The same bored cows grazed the fields. Angel wondered if they remembered her—how she and Bernie had stuck out their tongues and laughed. Probably not. Cows wouldn't care as long as they had grass to eat. They weren't like people, with feelings of lonesomeness and worrying about what might happen next. That was just people, wasn't it? Sure, you could scare a cow, but wouldn't they get over it as soon as you let them be? They didn't stand around fretting about the next scare and the next and the next.

She wondered for the millionth time where Bernie was and if he was scared. Was Verna taking good care of him, feeding him right, and making sure he was safe and happy? If only she could count on Verna to do it right. . . . And Wayne. Had she done the right thing, letting him go? Would she ever know what the right thing was? Well, Grandma wasn't doing the right thing, either, but at least Grandma knew she was messing up.

★   ★   ★   ★   ★

The nurse wouldn't let Miss Liza and her nephew see Ray. They weren't kin. Only kin could go into Intensive Care. Angel hadn't been in a hospital since she was born. They hadn't let her go to see Bernie when he was born. She had been too little. The smell was sharp and hurt her eyes, and when the nurse took her in to where Ray was, it was like some scene in a science-fiction horror movie. She had never properly seen the star man's face. It had always been dark without much moon, but there he lay, perfectly still against his pillows with wires and tubes stuck all over him. The only sound in the room was a weird whooshing. Someone had cut his hair and trimmed his beard close. His face lay grayish against the white linen, his lips were sunk and ridged. His eyes were closed. There was no way she would have taken him for the magical star man. This was Ray Morgan, or what was left of him. He looked shriveled, older than Grandma.

"You got a visitor, Mr. Morgan." The nurse's voice made Angel jump.

The face on the pillow turned toward her, and the eyes opened. "Angel," he said.

"Hi." She didn't know what to call him. She'd never called him anything out loud.

"Mama didn't come, I take it."

"She wasn't feeling too good."

He half smiled. "It's okay. You came." He closed his eyes again as though he was too tired to hold up his lids for any length of time.

She didn't know what to say next. She just stood there, wondering what you were supposed to say to a person lying in a hospital looking like he was about to die.

"I been missing you," she said finally.

"I been missing you, too," he said, opening his eyes again. "Listen. If I don't come through the operation tomorrow, I want you to have the telescope. Don't let anybody say different, okay? I don't want Mama selling it off."

"What do you mean? It's yours. You'll be needing it."

"No. Probably not."

She went cold all over. "You can't die," she said.

"I guess I can, Angel."

"I don't want you to die."

"I appreciate that. I'm not crazy to die myself, but I have a feeling I'm due."

"No." She said it stubbornly, angrily. He had no business dying.

"It's just my old worn-out body, Angel. I never treated it right, and now it's payback time."

"You're not as old as Grandma, and she's not about to die."

"Don't be mad at me, Angel. If I'd known you were coming back, I'd have taken better care of myself. It's too late now, but I'm grateful I lived long enough to point you at the stars."

"I don't know near enough! You gotta come back and teach me."

"You remember what I said last summer?"

"About what?"

"About us coming from the stars? About our bodies being made of the same stuff as the stars?"

"Yeah."

"Well, try to think about me going back to the stars where I belong, okay? Whenever you look at the stars, think about old Ray turned back to stardust."

"What about Grandma?"

"What about her?"

"She's going to feel terrible if you go die on her before she's had a chance to make it right with you. I know she is."

"Tell her she was a good mama to me. Tell her"—he paused and licked his cracked lips—"you tell her I love her. She'll believe you."

"I want you to tell her yourself."

"I will if I can, Angel. I might not have . . ."

He never finished the sentence. The nurse came in and told Angel her time was up, the patient had to rest. "I'll be back," she said. "You better be here when I do, you hear me?"

It was the last thing she ever said to him.

★ ★ ★ ★ ★

Miss Liza sent Eric to take them to the funeral. Angel was afraid Grandma would refuse to go, but she put on a black dress rusty with age and a patched overcoat and got into the car.

In front of the church was a long black hearse. Two men with slicked-down hair, wearing identical black double-breasted raincoats, were standing beside it. When Eric's car pulled up behind the hearse, the two men came over. One of them opened the door for Grandma to get out.

"I'm sorry for your loss, Mrs. Morgan."

Grandma didn't take the hand he offered, didn't even look at him. As he closed the door of Eric's old Buick, he said, "Mr. Morgan didn't arrange for a family limousine; otherwise, of course . . ."

The second man cleared his throat. "The casket is already at the gravesite," he said. "If you'll come this way." He took Grandma under the elbow. She shook him off.

Angel could see Miss Liza shuffling out the door of the library. "Wait, Grandma," she said. "Miss Liza's coming."

Eric ran over and took his great-aunt's hand. Angel, the undertakers, even Grandma stared at the librarian, her hand in her young nephew's, her head sidewise, her skinny little legs picking their way across the uneven lawn. It took an age for the old lady to get to where they stood. "I'm so sorry, Erma," she said, her voice breaking. "He was such a lovely man."

Grandma shook her head and mumbled something that might have been "Thank you," but Angel couldn't be sure.

Angel had imagined a funeral service like the ones she'd seen in movies, where the church was packed and people stood up and said nice things about the dead person. She thought she might even get the nerve to stand up and tell people that the star man was her friend, that he had taught her about the heavens. But they didn't go inside the white church with its tall, copper-colored steeple. They went directly to the cemetery on the other side of the building, where a fresh hole had been dug in the ground. On one side of the hole was a plain boxlike coffin with an American flag neatly folded on top, and on the other, a mound of moist dirt. Two men in work clothes stood a short distance away, leaning on shovels. The undertakers herded the tiny group of mourners to the casket. There were two folding chairs. Grandma was told quietly to sit in one and Miss Liza in the other.

There were only two other mourners. They wore
heavy plaid jackets, big red workmen's hands poking out
of the sleeves. Awkwardly, they came to Grandma's chair
and introduced themselves. They said they had worked
with Ray Morgan at the landfill. It was Miss Liza, not
Grandma, who thanked them for coming.

"He was a good man," one of them said, and the
other nodded in agreement. Everyone thought Ray
Morgan was a good man. Why hadn't Grandma been
able to see it?

A short, bald man in a flowing black robe came out of
the back of the church. He shook hands with each of
them, murmured something Angel didn't catch, then
opened a small black book and began to read out loud.

On this gray morning, with the late-autumn grass
brown beneath her feet, it was hard to imagine that the
star man lay in that box next to a gash in the cold earth.
The star man should have been buried at night with all
his stars dancing in attendance. She could believe that the
shriveled man she had visited in the hospital, Grandma's
son Ray Morgan, was dead, but how could she believe the
magical star man was gone forever?

While the minister kept reading, she looked around at
Morgan tombstones, some so old she could hardly make
out the names and dates. It was funny to think of people
being scared of graveyards. How could you be scared of a
place that felt so quiet? There were big trees among the
stones. The limbs were bare now, but she remembered

seeing them last summer with their broad, leafy branches, almost inviting you to climb up into their laps.

Angel stood behind Miss Liza and Grandma. Grandma never raised her eyes from the ground. She had hardly spoken since they got the news of Ray Morgan's death. It was a good thing he'd made his own arrangements. Angel wouldn't have known what to do about getting him buried, and Grandma wouldn't have been of any use. And they didn't need a special car to bring them to the cemetery, no matter what the undertaker thought.

Miss Liza was crying softly, dabbing her eyes with a handkerchief. She had loved Ray Morgan, Angel felt sure of that. Maybe she was more like a mother to him than Grandma had been. Angel was glad he'd had Miss Liza to go to. She must have been the one who had taught him about the stars and told him he was kin to them.

The preacher was still reading from his book. "'The Lord is my Shepherd,'" he began. Miss Liza and Eric joined in. They had the whole thing memorized. When they said something about the valley of the shadow of death, Grandma's shoulders began to shake. Angel reached out and grasped them tightly with both hands. She could feel the old woman's sobs through the wool of her overcoat, sobs so deep inside her that they couldn't even burst through to sound.

One of the undertakers took the flag off the coffin, and, when Grandma made no move to take it, he put it on her lap. Then he nodded at the men in work clothes, who came forward and lowered the coffin on ropes down into the grave. When it reached the bottom and the ropes were pulled up, the preacher stepped around the end of the dark hole and took a handful of dirt from the mound. He threw it onto Ray Morgan's coffin.

"Ashes to ashes," he said. "Dust to dust."

Tears filled Angel's eyes. She shook her head. *No,* she thought. *Astra to astra, stardust to stardust.*

TWENTY

Take Something Like a Star

Grandma, please, you've got to eat something."

Grandma lifted her chin from her chest and stared at Angel. Her eyes were lifeless. She was worse than she'd been when Bernie disappeared. Since the day they'd buried Ray, it was as though she'd dug a grave inside herself and was more dead than alive.

"Look, Grandma. I went to all the trouble to build up a good fire in the stove to make you some nice roast chicken, and you won't even come to the table." No response. "I even made mashed potatoes. What do you want me to do? Pick you up and carry you over here?"

"I never went to see him in the hospital." The old woman's face crumpled into her hands, and she began to cry.

"I'm sorry, Grandma." She went to the rocker and patted Grandma's shaking shoulder. "I'm really sorry, but if you don't eat, you'll die, and then where will I be? I need you."

The old woman snuffled. "Horsefeathers," she muttered. "When did you ever need anybody?"

"No. It's the truth. I *do* need you. And what if—what

if Bernie called, and you weren't here and Welfare has already taken me off somewhere? What would Bernie do then?" She shook Grandma's shoulder. "You got a responsibility, Grandma!"

"You got a lot of nerve." Grandma pulled out a dingy handkerchief and blew her nose. "Well, help me up, girl. I'm stiff as starch."

Grandma played with her food, but by begging and cajoling and threatening, Angel managed to get the old woman to take three bites of chicken and a spoonful of mashed potatoes. "Where's the gravy?" Grandma asked.

"If you eat two bites more, I promise you I'll make gravy tomorrow, okay? I swear, it's worse'n trying to make Bernie eat."

"Hmmph." Grandma gave a tiny hint of a grin.

★ ★ ★ ★ ★

She didn't mention the telescope to Grandma. She thought it better to wait for a while before talking about Ray's things, still over in the trailer. Besides, she didn't know how heavy it was, or whether she'd even be able to carry it from the trailer to the house. The first clear night after Ray's death, she visited the field. She knew he wouldn't be there. Still, something inside half hoped to see the star man.

It was a perfect night for viewing. He wasn't there, of course, but with her naked eye she picked out the great Andromeda Galaxy. If good people went to heaven when they died, that's where the star man would be—in that glorious cluster. He might be two million miles away, but he would always be there, burning bright among the stars of another galaxy.

"Hi, star man," she whispered. "It's me, Angel. I won't ever forget you. Promise."

★ ★ ★ ★ ★

Little by little, Grandma came back to life. "I'm too mean to die," she said, which was probably true. She'd gotten along all that time on canned beans and peaches, hadn't she? Angel hated to leave her, but she had to go to school on weekdays and to the store and the library on Saturdays.

Miss Liza could be counted on to get her good books, including short, funny picture books that she could read aloud to Grandma. Sometimes she lingered longer than she should have talking to Miss Liza. They'd talk about Ray Morgan, about how he'd longed to go to college and become an astronomer but went, instead, to war, and in that short time lived through so much killing he drugged himself for years afterward, trying to dull the pain of all that horror.

Grandma was always grumpy when she was later than usual, suspecting that it was Miss Liza who had detained her, but Angel needed that time with the librarian more than she needed almost anything. On the Saturday after Ray's burial, Miss Liza read her his favorite poem. It was by a man named Robert Frost, who had lived in Vermont in the years when Ray was young.

The man was talking to a star, not wishing on a star but asking the star questions, as though he wanted to know what it was like to be a star, then finally realizing that the star wasn't explaining itself but asking something of *him*.

> *"'Not even stooping from its sphere,*
> *It asks a little of us here.*
> *It asks of us a certain height,*
> *So when at times the mob is swayed*
> *To carry praise or blame too far,*
> *We may take something like a star*
> *To stay our minds on and be staid.'"*

"What does it mean?" she asked Miss Liza. "I don't understand."

"I think you do," said Miss Liza. "I think you understand better than almost anyone I know how to manage when other people are blaming you or making fun of you or letting you down. I think you know to fix your mind on a star, to be strong and stand tall."

Angel looked at the bent-over little woman, and the words "stand tall" seemed strange but true, and although she thought Miss Liza was giving her too much credit— Angel could think all too often of the times she had been weak and close to dissolving in despair—it was something to live up to, wasn't it? No matter what other people did or failed to do, you could try yourself to be something like Polaris, shining strong and bright and fixed in a swirling world of darkness.

She asked Miss Liza to let her take the poetry book home. She wanted to read the poem over and over again. She might never understand it, she knew; still she wanted it to be inside her, a part of her star stuff.

★   ★   ★   ★   ★

As soon as Angel turned up the driveway, she saw the car. Not a brand-new one, but almost clean, not like most of the cars out here in the country. Her stomach did a flip-flop even before she saw the middle-aged, neatly dressed woman sitting at the wheel. They'd found her. She almost made a dash for it, but it would be hard to get far carrying a book and a bag of groceries. Anyhow, it was already too late. The woman had spotted her and was getting out of the car.

"Hello, Angel," she said. "I'm Mrs. Morris."

Angel clutched Robert Frost more tightly in her left hand and propped the bulky bag she held in her right arm on her hip. "Hi," she said.

"Here"—the woman reached out—"Let me help you with that load."

"It's okay. I can manage." She could see out of the corner of her eye that Grandma was standing on the front porch and watching. "Did you want to see my grandma?"

"I've already met her. Actually, you're the person I was waiting to see." She looked around the junk-filled yard.

"Is there somewhere we could talk—just the two of us? The sugar shack, maybe?"

Angel shook her head. Her mouth felt frozen. So this was the way it was going to be. She cleared her throat. "It's . . . sort of filled with stuff. Storage, you know." *Does a messy shed count against you? One your daddy hid in?*

"Would you mind just sitting in the car, then?"

She did mind. You never knew when you got into a social worker's car, where you would end up, but the woman had already opened the rear door and was reaching for the groceries. "Here," she said. "Why don't you just set that heavy bag in here and then jump in the front seat with me? The law won't fuss about a minor in the front seat as long as the car isn't moving." She laughed as though she'd made a joke.

Angel put the groceries in back and went around to the front seat. She left the door open. Not that she was going to make a run for it, but just so she wouldn't feel trapped. She held on to Robert Frost the way Bernie used to hold on to Grizzle. *To stay your mind on and be staid.*

"What's your book?" the social worker asked.

"Just some poetry."

"That's nice." The woman was quiet for a moment, thrumping a silent rhythm on the steering wheel, looking ahead through the windshield. "We've got a problem here, Angel," she began.

You've got a problem. I'm fine.

"Did you know your father said he walked away from his work crew because he was hoping to see you?"

Work crew? She didn't try to answer. She might betray herself.

"Well, that's what he told the police when they finally caught up with him—that he was trying to check up on you. He said that the reason he took off was that you had called him. You were all upset, he said, because your mother had taken your brother away and left you alone here with your great-grandmother."

So that business about parole had been a lie. Angel bit her lip. She mustn't speak. Not even to ask if they knew where Bernie was.

"We haven't been able to locate your mother or your brother, but we did need to see about you. We had no idea your mother had deserted you."

"I'm fine here. Grandma and I are getting along real well."

"Well, your dad didn't have a lot of good things to say about his grandmother. Of course, we know how families are sometimes . . ." She was still looking straight ahead, holding tightly to the wheel.

"Daddy's mad because of something that happened years ago. That's why he told the police about Mama. He's mad at her for not sticking by him when he was in jail. He's probably mad at me, too." The words were out of her mouth before she knew it.

The woman gave her a sharp look. "He has no reason

to be mad at you, Angel. For all his faults, I think your father cares about you. He wants to make sure you're all right." She seemed to be searching Angel's profile for lies. "He doesn't believe your great-grandmother is capable—"

Angel looked her straight in the face. "Yes, she is. I swear to God. We do good together. You can ask anybody."

"But that's just it, Angel. Just who can I ask?"

"Well, you can ask me, or Grandma. We're the ones who know best, aren't we?"

"Angel, a couple of years ago one of our people asked you about your mother. Remember what you said? You said she'd turned herself around and was going to be a great mom for you and Bernie." She was quiet a minute, staring hard into Angel's eyes. "I'm not sure you're the best judge, sweetie."

"You can't take me away. Please. You can't."

"I don't want to, Angel, but it's my job to make sure you're safe, and hopefully"—she gave Angel a crooked smile—"happy."

Happy. Sappy. Grandma was holding on to one of the porch pillars, her face shrunk into prune lines. She looked like something might blow her away if she didn't hold on for all she was worth. *Stand up, Grandma. She'll see you over there caving in on yourself like a black hole.* "There is somebody knows us both who can tell you how good we're doing."

"Someone close by that you see on a regular basis?"

"Yeah. Miss Liza Irwin. Grandma and her have been friends all their lives, and she's been friends with me ever since I came last summer. We—I see her on a very regular basis, and Grandma just saw her last week." *No need to add it was at a funeral and the first time in about a hundred years.*

"Where can I find this friend of yours?"

"She runs the library. She's a librarian. All her family's been librarians. The library's that little house in the village between the store and the church. It's got a big sign with her name painted right on it. You can't miss it." Angel was already getting out of the car. She gave the door a satisfying bang before retrieving her grocery bag from the backseat. With a swing of her hip, she pushed the rear door shut. "Miss Liza Irwin," Angel called to the woman through the closed window. "She's a leading citizen."

The woman rolled down the window partway. "I get your message, Angel. Don't worry. I'll pay Miss Irwin a visit on my way back." She wound up the window and started the motor.

"And tell Daddy I'm doing great, okay?" Angel was yelling now, smiling crazily, almost jumping up and down to prove how very healthy and happy she was as she ran toward the porch where Grandma still sagged like a whipped dog. She put her free arm around Grandma's shoulder and waved. The woman nodded at them both through the windshield and began to back up.

"She gonna take you away from me, Angel?"

"Nah." Angel shifted the heavy grocery bag, watching the car turn and head out the driveway. "Nah. I'm siccing Miss Liza on her. She won't know what hit her. Could you open the door, Grandma? I'm 'bout to drop this bag."

"What are you talking about, girl? You told her to talk to Liza Irwin? No telling what that woman will say about me!"

"Open the door, *please*."

Grandma opened it, following anxiously behind. "Liza Irwin? I can't believe you. You know what that crooked old thing's liable to say about me?"

Angel put the bag on the table. "She'll say I got a terrific grandma and I'm lucky as heck to get to live with you."

"She'll say nothing of the sort! Liza Irwin knows good and well I've hated her guts since I was six years old."

"She won't say nice things because she *likes* you, Grandma. She'll say them because she's Liza Irwin. Liza Irwin is just like George Washington. She cannot tell a lie."

Grandma sputtered. "See? That's exactly what I mean. How can you *not* hate someone too perfect to tell a lie?"

TWENTY-ONE

Shining Stars

It was nearly Thanksgiving when Bernie finally called, and neither of them was ready. "Angel," his little voice said. "Come get me. Please."

"Bernie! Where are you?"

"In the hospital. I'm hurt."

"What's the matter?"

"Just come get me, Angel. I want to come home with you."

She cupped her hand over the receiver. "Grandma," she said. "It's Bernie."

"I ain't deaf. Where is he?"

"What hospital, Bernie?"

"I don't know."

"Ask somebody. Is Mama there?"

"She's here somewhere, but I don't know where."

"Bernie. Call the nurse. I need to talk to the nurse."

"I want to come to Grandma's house."

"I know, Bernie. But we can't come get you if we don't know where you are. Call the nurse so I can talk to her. Now. Please."

She could hear him yelling at the other end of the line.

Someone told him roughly to keep his voice down, and what was he doing using the phone without permission, then, in a quite different tone of voice, "Hello. Who am I speaking to?"

"This is Bernie Morgan's sister," Angel said.

"Is there an adult that I can speak to?"

"Grandma. They want a grownup."

Grandma heaved herself out of the rocker. "Yeah?" she shouted into the phone.

The call consisted mostly of high-pitched, undecipherable conversation on the other end and "eh-yups" on Grandma's end. Finally, when Angel thought she would bust a gut if it went on another second, Grandma said a final "eh-yup" and hung up the phone.

"Well, where is he? What happened?"

Grandma sighed as she hung up the receiver. "They're over to Barre. Where Ray was."

"How bad is it?"

"Bernie's bunged up, sounds like. But he's like me, too mean to die."

"What about Mama?"

Grandma shook her head. "I don't know. The guy had been drinking . . ."

"What guy?"

"Hell, how should I know? One of her boyfriends, I guess."

"Did he beat them up?"

"They didn't say that. They was in a car. It was a car wreck."

"She never fastens her seat belt or Bernie's. I told her and told her!"

"Calm down. Yelling ain't gonna help nothing." She started for her chair. "I guess you need to sweet-talk little Miss Perfect into getting us a ride."

★   ★   ★   ★   ★

It was several frantic hours before Miss Liza could locate her nephew. Still more time passed before Eric was able to get off work to drive over and collect them. "Do you want me to come along?" Miss Liza asked.

What should she say? Of course she wanted Miss Liza to come, but Angel was afraid that if she did, Grandma was liable not to go at all. "She's really grateful about the social worker, about you giving her such a great recommendation and all. I don't know. It's just seems hard for her to—"

"Angel?"

"Yeah?"

"Maybe I shouldn't. Right?"

"I'm sorry. She really is grateful to you—she just has a hard time showing it."

"No, no. I understand. You mustn't worry. Eric will be there within a half hour. Give Bernie my love."

Both Angel and Grandma rode in the backseat of Eric's old Buick as though they were strangers riding in a taxi, not speaking to each other, much less to Eric. *Are they going to be all right? Oh, God, why wouldn't she listen to me? You never ride with someone's been drinking. You always buckle your seat belt.* When they finally got to the hospital, Eric said, "I'll just park and wait for you in the lobby, okay?"

"Thanks," Angel said. Grandma had yet to say a word.

She was the one who had to talk to the man volunteering on the Information Desk. He had a gray fringe of hair and a little toothbrush mustache, which kept wiggling as he screwed his mouth to punch information into the computer. He stopped and stared at the screen. "I got two Morgans listed," the man said, as though that were a real puzzle.

"That's right. Bernie and Verna," said Angel.

"Are you close relatives?" He eyed them suspiciously.

"I'm Verna's daughter, and Bernie's my brother. This is our grandma."

He kept staring at the computer as though it might call her a liar.

"You heard the girl," Grandma snapped. "What rooms they in?"

The man sniffed. "Bernie Morgan is in Children's, but Mrs. Verna Morgan is in the ICU. That's immediate family members only." Angel's body went cold. The star man had been in the ICU. That's where they put you if you were going to die. Her mouth was too dry to speak.

"Well," said Grandma. "We're 'bout as 'mediate as you can get. We'll go see the boy first. Where's he at?"

Going up in the elevator Grandma went quiet again, fiddling with the broken clasp of her pocketbook. Angel stuck her index finger in her mouth and chewed on the nail. *Oh, Bernie, Bernie, please be all right.* When they got to the floor, they both hesitated so long that the door began to close before they moved. Angel grabbed the rubber edge and held on to it until they could both get off.

Dread was weighing down her chest like an iron bar as she searched above the doors for the number the volunteer had given them. "This is it," she said, more to herself than to Grandma. She took a deep, shuddering breath and stepped into the room.

Bernie was propped up in the bed nearest the window, watching television. His right leg was dangling from the ceiling in a kind of pulley. Intent on the screen mounted on the wall, he didn't see Angel until she was right next to his bed.

"Hi, Bernie."

His head whipped around. "I thought you wasn't ever going to come. I waited and waited and waited."

"We came as soon as we could, Bernie. We had to get a ride, you know."

"I bet you don't know how I got Grandma's number."

"No, I was wondering about that."

"I called nine-one-one."

"Bernie! That's for emergencies only!"

"It *was* an emergency. I didn't know your number. The lady was very nice, too."

"I'll write it down for you."

"Too late. After you made me call the nurse, they took

the phone away." He stuck his lip out in a pout. "Now I can't call you again."

"Well, don't worry. We're here now." Angel reached out to touch his thin arm. "Say hello to Grandma." Grandma was still standing in the doorway as though afraid to come closer.

"I was just going to, Angel. You don't have to tell me everything, you know. Hi, Grandma," he called out over the sound of the TV. "My leg's all busted."

She took a baby step into the room. "Yeah." She straightened up and came toward the bed. "Eh-yup. I knew there must be some explanation. Nobody would have thought you was pretty enough to hang up like a picture."

Bernie started to giggle but stopped himself. "I got hurt really bad," he said. "They won't even let Mama come visit me, I'm so bad off."

"You just bad, period," Grandma said.

"I am not."

"Hoo, boy, don't you try to fool me. I know you. Hand me that chair, Angel." When Angel got the chair and put it close by the head of Bernie's bed, Grandma plopped down in it. "So's this TV any good?"

Mama. Angel'd almost forgotten in her relief on seeing Bernie. She hoped they'd let her into the ICU without a grownup, but anyhow, she had to try. "You guys behave, okay? I'll be back in a minute." She slipped out of the room without waiting for an answer.

★ ★ ★ ★ ★

"Excuse me. I need to see my mom," she said to the bowed-over head at the nurses' station. When the nurse lifted her head, Angel remembered her. "You took care of my uncle Ray," she said. "Ray Morgan?"

"You're the little Morgan girl, aren't you?" The nurse shook her head. She got up and came around the circular desk. "Sometimes trouble comes piling in, doesn't it, honey?" She put her arm around Angel and took her gently down to where Verna lay.

Maybe seeing Verna in Intensive Care wasn't as big a shock as it had been when the star man had been lying there like someone out of a science-fiction horror movie. Though it seemed worse to see Verna with no makeup, her face swollen and bruised as if she'd been in a prize-fight. She'd dyed her hair red sometime since summer, but it lay lank and greasy against the white pillow. Wires and tubes grew out of her body like strange colored vines. There were green ones coming out of her nose.

"Just a few minutes, okay, honey?" the nurse said. "We don't want to wear her out."

Angel nodded. She forced herself close to the bed. "Mama," she said.

Verna turned toward the sound. It looked as though it took all the strength she could manage just to turn and open her swollen eyes, so there was none left for her voice. "Angel?"

"Yeah, it's me. How you doing?"

"Not so good. You seen Bernie?"

"Yeah. Just now. He's doing fine. He's watching TV and talking to Grandma."

"How—how did you know we—?"

"Bernie called. We came as soon as we could get a ride."

"I'm sorry, Angel. About everything . . ."

"Don't worry about it, Mama. I'm doing okay, and Bernie's gonna be all right. You just think about getting better yourself."

"I keep messing up, don't I? You and Bernie would be better off if . . ."

"Me and Bernie need you, Mama. You don't know how much I been missing you."

"I didn't want to leave you, Angel, but this guy I was with, well, he wasn't crazy about having one kid, much less two." She turned her head away. "I should have left Bernie with you. You'd have kept him safe." Verna's cracked lips parted into a half smile. "You always was a better mom than me."

"You want some water?" There was a glass with a bent straw on the table near the bed. Angel got it and put the straw between Verna's lips. Verna raised her head a few inches and took a sip.

"Thanks, baby," she said, lying back, her eyes closed.

She's going to give up! She thinks she can just let go and leave everything to me. Well, she can't. Not this time. Angel put the glass down. She cleared her throat. "Mama, listen. We'll take Bernie home as soon as they let him out. But you gotta promise to come, too—as soon as you can. We all want you to come."

"Even Grandma?"

"Especially Grandma. She's so worn out trying to be the grownup she don't know what end's up."

"I thought you was the grownup, baby. You always have been."

"I'm even more tired of being the grownup than Grandma is. I'm not even twelve years old, Mama. I'm not supposed to be the grownup. That's your job."

"I might not get the chance, Angel." She lifted a hand, with a tube attached, about an inch and then let it drop weakly onto the sheet. "I'm messed up pretty bad inside—"

"You get well, you hear? You don't have any right wimping out on us. You're the mother!"

"Okay, baby," she said. "I'll try. Promise."

Angel wanted to cry. The tears were burning in her eyes, but she wasn't going to go soft. Verna *had* to get well, and tears might make Verna think she could give up, quit trying. Angel wasn't about to give her leave to do that.

"I'm telling you, Verna Morgan, I don't want any of your promises. You *gotta* get well and come home. I'm not going to let you do anything else. You hear?"

"Okay," she said, a flicker of a smile on her dry lips. "Okay, baby. You're the boss."

"I am *not* the boss. I'm just the kid. Hear?"

"I hear you." She was really smiling now, her eyes open, with a spark of something like life in them.

★ ★ ★ ★ ★

An inch or two of snow had fallen during the day, lending the junk-filled yard a frosted elegance. After she had shoveled a path a few feet from the house into the yard, Angel carried a kitchen chair out and put the quilt from Bernie's bed on it. Bernie's leg was still weak, and he couldn't stand for too long at a time, but it was going to be a night starry enough for Galileo Galilei, and she needed to share it with him. She helped him hobble out the door and sit down. Then she wrapped the quilt around him.

"You're not too cold, are you?"

"Nah," he said. "I like it out here." He looked around him at the snow-covered humps of discarded junk and then up at the star-spattered sky. "Wish on the star, Angel!" he said, pointing.

"That's not a star, Bernie. It's a planet."

"It is, too, a star, and I'm going to wish on it, and you can't stop me."

There was no need to give Bernie lessons in astronomy tonight—no use, really. "What are you wishing for, Bernie?"

"That when Mama comes home tomorrow, she won't ever go away again."

"That's a good wish."

"What do you wish for, Angel?"

"I wish we'd all be happy together—you and me and Mama and Grandma and Miss Liza and Eric and—"

"And Daddy, too?"

She took a deep breath. "Yeah," she said. "Daddy, too."

"You 'member when I wished he wouldn't ever come home?"

"Yeah."

"That was bad, wasn't it?"

"Well, you hardly know him. He's been in jail so long."

"I bet he likes me better than Jake did."

"Who's Jake?"

"The one that made the wreck."

"Oh."

"He was always mad that Mama come and got me."

"Was he mean to you?" she asked fearfully.

"Some. I didn't like him." She didn't dare ask him what he meant. She couldn't stand it if some strange man had beat up on him. "Would Daddy be mean to me?" he asked.

"He never hit me a single time when I was little. Remember? I told you he was the one gave me Grizzle."

"Oh, yeah."

"He messed up a lot, maybe he still does sometimes, but he was never mean to me or you, either. I think—I know he really loves us."

"That's good," Bernie said, stretching out his leg.

"Your leg hurt?"

"Some," he said. "When Mama gets all well, we should go back to the jail and see him, shouldn't we?"

"Yeah, after she's all well and strong, yeah, we ought to ask her about that."

"Angel?"

"Yes, Bernie?"

"I missed you when I was gone."

"I missed you, too, Bernie."

"I thought it would be nice to have Mama to myself, but it was all wrong. I didn't like it without you there."

Angel swallowed hard. "We need to stick together, Bernie. We're a family."

"Yeah," he said.

"Are you cold?" she asked again. She'd wrapped him up as best she could, but the December air bit and stung.

"Some," he said.

"Want to go in?"

He shook his head. "Not yet." They were both quiet for a long time, looking at the sky. "Angel," he said at last, "what makes the stars shine?"

"They're on fire, Bernie."

"Oh," he said, the fire of the stars sparkling in his eyes.

Acknowledgments

Special thanks must go to Kathy Searles, for sharing her knowledge of the Vermont correctional system and of the families whose lives are bound up in the system, and to Bob Merrill, who acted as my star man for this book. Any errors that remain are mine alone.

The books on stars that Angel loves are: H. A. Rey's *Know the Stars*, originally published by Houghton Mifflin Company in 1954. Angel checked out from the library an abridged paperback edition published by Scholastic Book Services in 1969. *Starry Messenger* by Peter Sís was published by Farrar, Straus and Giroux in 1996 and received a Caldecott Honor the following year.

Bernie's favorite books are by Harry Allard with pictures by James Marshall. *The Stupids Step Out,* the book Miss Liza first reads to him, was published in 1974 by Houghton Mifflin Company.

Robert Frost's poem, "Take Something Like a Star," is from *The Poetry of Robert Frost,* edited by Edward Connery Lathem and published by Henry Holt in paperback in 1979.

And, as ever, thanks to Virginia Buckley and John Paterson, without whose help and encouragement this book would never have been published.

Warlands

No one really knew the true story of Uncle Ho's early life before he came to Amy's family. All they knew was that he was a Vietnamese orphan, born among the bombings and terrors of war. But the warland nightmares in Uncle Ho's head won't go away.

'...a very thoughtful and original exploration of the function of storytelling itself and its power to stretch, bind and liberate. Warlands is one of the most thoughtful and compelling novels for this age group I've read in ages.'
SCHOOL LIBRARIAN JOURNAL

Rachel Anderson

Rachel Anderson has worked in Radio and newspaper journalism and in 1991 won the Medical Journalist's Association Award. Rachel won the Guardian Children's Fiction Award for *Paper Faces*. When not writing she is involved with the needs and care of children who are socially and mentally challenged.

Unique

 Shortlisted for the Branford Boase Award, Angus Book Award, Booktrust Teenage Prize, the South Lanarkshire Award, and the North East Book Award

Dominic finds a photograph in his granddad's loft. When his parents refuse to tell him anything, Dominic starts to seek out the truth for himself. Uncovering a horrific secret he unleashes a chain of events that will have far reaching and disastrous consequences.

'A terrific book – exciting, heartening, intelligent and all too topical ... ★★★★★*'*
BOOKS FOR KEEPS

Alison Allen-Gray
After gaining a BA Hons in English and Drama at University of Wales, Alison co-founded a performing arts centre, converted from on old cinema, on the south coast of England. She has co-written two children's musicals and one for adults while developing her acting career, mainly in children's theatre.

River Boy

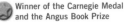 Winner of the Carnegie Medal and the Angus Book Prize

Grandpa is dying. He can barely move his hands any more, but stubborn as ever, refuses to stay in hospital. He's determined to finish his last painting, 'River Boy', before he goes. A poignant story that explores the subject of grief and loss in an accessible and affecting way.

'River Boy has all the hallmarks of a classic – it deepens with re-reading and takes the readers on a journey. You are not the same person at the end of this book.'
CARNEGIE JUDGES

Tim Bowler

Tim Bowler is an experienced class room teacher, becoming Head of Modern Languages before leaving to become a full-time freelance writer and translator. Tim has won numerous awards for his novels, including the prestigious Carnegie Medal.

Calling a Dead Man

When John, an explosives expert, dies in an accident in Russia, his sister Hayley and friend Annie go there to mourn. Before long they begin to suspect that there is more to John's death than meets the eye and that certain people are desperately trying to keep them away from the truth.

'This complex thriller demands staying power, but in the hands of this writer, it's well worth the roller-coaster of a ride.'
GUARDIAN CHILDREN'S BOOK SUPPLEMENT

Gillian Cross

Gillian Cross has been writing children's books for over 20 years, and she has won not only the Carnegie Medal for *Wolf* but also the Smarties Prize and the Whitbread Children's Novel Award for *The Great Elephant Chase*. Gillian's *Demon Headmaster* has been serialized on BBC television.

The Lastling

 Shortlisted for the Calderdale Children's Book Award

Paris is thrilled when her Uncle Franklin decides to take her with him on his trip to the Himalayas. Franklin's influence gets them into places where tourists are not allowed, even into the forbidden war-zone, deep in the forest, to look for exotic and endangered species. Franklin is a man with a vision, something dark and strange, but just how strange, Paris is about to find out...

Philip Gross

Philip Gross has won several prizes for his poetry and his collection *The Wasting Game* was shortlisted for the Whitbread Poetry Award. He is now Professor of Creative Writing at the University of Glamorgan.

The Merrybegot

 Nominated for Guardian Children's Fiction Award 2005

Nell lives with her grandmother, the local cunning woman and healer, in a seventeenth century West Country village. When one of the minister's daughters falls pregnant she and her sister attempt to conceal it by accusing Nell of putting a curse on them. Nell is alone, trapped and in mortal danger. Who can she trust? Who will save her?

A gripping, atmospheric novel, which demands reading at one sitting. Five Stars'
BOOKS FOR KEEPS

Julie Hearn

Julie Hearn worked as a journalist before completing a Masters in Women's Studies at Oxford University. An idea for her Masters thesis became the inspiration for *Follow Me Down*, Julie's first novel.